# The Seven Pillars of Tarook

## The Guardians of Elestra #4

### Thom Jones

Peekaboo Pepper Books

# DEDICATION

This book is dedicated to Galen, Aidan, Linda, and Dinara. Aidan reads and rereads each book so many times and finds mistakes that I miss each time. Galen likes to suggest new sections just before the books are done, and I think they always make the stories better. My wife Linda is my main editor. She's not afraid to cross whole sections out and give me ideas for better ways to say things. Dinara's too young to read the books yet, but she makes me realize that I'll have a dedicated reader for the rest of Derek's and Deanna's adventures in Elestra.

The Seven Pillars of Tarook, Guardians of Elestra #4

Also available in the Guardians of Elestra series:

To learn more about Elestra, including maps, history, Tobungus' blog, Glabber's menu, and contests that allow readers to submit ideas for new characters, places, or other magical things, please visit:

www.guardiansofelestra.com

# CONTENTS

# 1 Assuming the Worst

Deanna Hughes woke up early. At least, she thought it was early. "Derek?" she mumbled, wondering whether her twin brother was still sleeping.

"Yeah, Deanna?" Derek answered from across the room, where he sat looking out the window. "The sun just came up about ten minutes ago. I didn't expect you to wake up for an hour or two."

"Why are you up?" she asked, still shaking the web of sleep from her mind.

"I've been getting up early lately," he answered.

"Are you alright?" She was worried that he was getting depressed about being away from their parents. They had been transported to the magical world of Elestra where they were racing to find the powerful moonstones before the dark wizard Eldrack could get his hands on them. They had made new friends, including Tobungus, the mushroom man, and Zorell, a talking cat. These two seemed to hate each other, which often led to entertaining arguments.

They also spent time with two powerful wizards, Iszarre and Glabber. Iszarre was a human wizard who also worked as a cook at Glabber's Grub Hut. They had found out that Iszarre was a trained chef and that the snake wizard Glabber was a leading wizard from the Desert Realm.

Over the past three days, Derek and Deanna had explored Amemnop. They went to museums, tiny magic shops, cafes, and bakeries. They bought Elestran clothes and ate lots of new foods, some good and some not so good. At one magic shop, Deanna bought three lemons, and Derek bought a collection of green-flamed candles for his story scroll.

The most unusual place they visited was the Magian Zoo and Bestiary where bizarre creatures from all over Elestra were paid to live and tell visitors about themselves. After looking at the directory of creatures at the zoo, Derek and Deanna sat down for a nice long talk with a knifebird.

Eldrack had used knifebirds to attack them in the Desert Realm where they found the third moonstone. They wanted to know why the knifebirds followed Eldrack. Their earlier research on Eldrack's minions revealed that some of the groups following Eldrack had been angry at King Barado because of disagreements over music.

The knifebird told them that a flock of knifebirds had flown to the Antikrom Mountains to sell extra feathers, which could be used to absorb magical liquids, such as healing potions or sleep juice, to be used later. A terrible storm rose up unexpectedly and blew the birds into a thick forest where they became lost. Eldrack found them and told them that if they helped him on an expedition, he would lead them to safety. The birds were so thankful that they joined Eldrack's army.

After the knifebird had told them all that he knew about Eldrack, the large bird was no longer scary to the twins. They had learned about his people and realized that the knifebirds were not really bad. It was more like they were loyal. As a parting gift, he gave them each a feather for their adventures yet to come

As Deanna thought again about Derek waking up early, she thought back on all they had done, but realized that sometimes even all of Elestra's uniqueness was not enough to stop them from missing their parents and their home.

"Oh, yeah, I'm fine," Derek said, knowing that Deanna thought he was getting homesick. "Being here alone is getting easier, actually." He got up and moved closer to the window and continued. "I just can't get the prophecy out of my mind.  Can it be true that we'll join Eldrack?"

"No way!" Deanna nearly yelled. "Absolutely not!"

"Well, the prophecy seemed pretty sure," he said, still looking out the window.  Before going to the Desert Realm to find the third moonstone, he had gone to the Archive of Prophecies where an ancient woman named Gula Badu showed him a prophecy that appeared in a candle's flame.  He was concerned because the prophecy's last line was:

> *Following a terrible act of betrayal, the young wizards, first the sister, then the brother, will join their sworn enemy in the final battle.*

"I'm telling you, Derek.  We won't ever join Eldrack."  Deanna realized that Derek had been more worried about the prophecy than he had said.  She was suddenly wide awake.  "We've seen what he's done.  He has so many generations of our family in those awful tubes in the Cave of Imprisonment, and he's after us."  She shuddered, remembering their grandfather with the white fog circling him in his tube.

"Is he really, Deanna?" Derek asked, turning from the window to look at her.  Before she could reply, he continued, "He's powerful.  There's no doubt about that. He knows Elestra better than we do. He's had his chances if he wanted to capture us. Why hasn't he?"

"Maybe he needs us to get the moonstones," she said. "He's always trying to steal them from us."

"But why do we need to get the moonstones instead of him?" Derek asked. "He's strong enough to do the things we've done."

"I'll agree that he is strong," Deanna said. "Hmm. Maybe each Mystical Guardian put a protective spell on the moonstones when they were hidden so that they could only be found by other Mystical Guardians."

"Well, Iszarre never said anything about that," Derek said. "But, there's a lot that Iszarre hasn't said. It's like he wants us to figure things out on our own."

"That would make sense. We've learned that some magic is affected by talking about it," Deanna said. "It's like those prophecies where you're not supposed to talk about them. Remember, when we were in the Desert Realm, how Dahlia didn't want to talk about the prophecy in her grandmother's house? It was about us, and she knew that if she talked about it, everything could change."

Derek nodded as Deanna spoke. She

continued, "Maybe Iszarre can't tell us about the Mystical Guardians' spells because telling us would break the spells."

Derek was thinking about the moonstones they had found. He finally said, "It's possible that the Mystical Guardians put protective spells on the moonstones, but Tobungus was the one who found the second stone in the Baroka Valley."

"But I was the one who popped the stone out of the stain-glass window," Deanna interrupted.

"So, it's possible," Derek said. "But, I'm still not sure."

"Okay, maybe he's trying to trick us," Deanna suggested. "Maybe he wants us to stop fearing him, or even to trust him. Then, when he makes his move for the moonstones, he can try to get our help. Does that sound possible?"

"Yeah, I was actually thinking that," Derek replied. "You know, like he thinks he can trick us."

Deanna could see that there was still concern in Derek's eyes. "We'll just have to be careful, Derek."

"I think we're missing something, Deanna," Derek said quietly.

"All that I'm missing right now is breakfast," Deanna said, trying to lighten the mood.

"Well, I'm sure that Glabber will have

something interesting for us to eat this morning," Derek said, pushing his concern to the side.

Deanna got dressed and gathered the wand, a flashlight, and a few other things to put in her backpack. After making sure that they hadn't forgotten anything, they walked down to the diner below. Glabber's Grub Hut was busy, even at such an early hour, but that didn't stop the great serpent chef from slithering over to their table as soon as they sat down. Glabber took a long look at the children and hissed, "A special breakfast will do you some good."

"What do you mean?" Derek asked.

"Young man," Glabber hissed, "I have been in Amemnop during the dark times before you broke Eldrack's spell. I have seen the dark clouds of fear, worry, and anger shroud the faces of enough people to know that you are consumed by thoughts of something mysterioussssssss." His eyes glowed a golden yellow as the last word rolled slowly off of his forked tongue.

"He's alright, Glabber," Deanna said, "It's just that he can't stop thinking about a prophecy that suggested that we might . . . do something bad at the end of our quest."

"Prophecies are like looking into a rippling lake," Glabber said. "You see a reflection on the surface, but you don't know exactly what you are seeing, what lies beneath the surface. The words may be obscured by the ripples of the meaning that you think you read."

"I don't know. It seemed pretty clear," Derek replied.

"All prophecies do," Glabber hissed. "There is much more for you to learn before you can even try to understand the meaning of a prophecy such as this." He began to slither back to the kitchen. "I will get your breakfast, and Iszarre can help you understand more about prophecies."

A moment later, the great wizard Iszarre, wearing a flowing purple robe under his grimy apron, dropped into a chair across from Deanna. "What's this I hear about a prophecy?" he asked.

Deanna wanted to keep the actual prophecy secret, so she said, "Derek's just a little bit worried about a prophecy he read. It might have suggested that we would not succeed in our quest."

"My dear Deanna," Iszarre said with his eyes twinkling mysteriously, "Let me tell you something about prophecies." He stroked his chin. "Many, many years ago, I read the words of a prophecy in a candle's flame. It foretold of an epic struggle that I would face. It said that my wand, my greatest weapon, would be unable to help me."

Deanna sat forward. "What happened?"

"I prepared for months," Iszarre said seriously. "I practiced every defensive spell I knew, and I even tried to make up some new ones. I dreamt about magic at night and hummed songs about my spells during the day."

His look darkened. "Then one day, I was in the kitchen at a restaurant where I was working, when three men wearing dark robes walked in through the front door."

He could see that Deanna's attention was fixed on him. "I had thirty pancakes on the griddle, and I had just set my spatula wand in the jar with all of my other kitchen tools. I was rushing to finish everything, and I knocked over a jar of Blastolian sugarbush nectar. The nectar is the stickiest substance in Elestra. It oozed into the jar of utensils. My wand was stuck. So were the pancake turners."

"Is that when the dark wizards came into the kitchen?" Deanna asked.

"You see, Deanna," Iszarre said, "You have fallen for the trap of any prophecy. You expected a battle with dark wizards. To be fair," he chuckled, "that is what I expected."

He sat back in his chair. "However, those men were simply hungry Fradoolian crab traders. The real battle turned out to be with the thirty pancakes that were starting to burn on the griddle. I couldn't get my wand. What could I do?"

"Okay, so that was a goofy prophecy," Derek said. "Our prophecy seemed more serious."

"Derek, you don't understand how important my prophecy was," Iszarre replied.

"I don't mean to be rude, but I don't think that a battle with thirty burning pancakes can compare to joining Eldrack," Derek said, and then realized that he let the terrible part of the prophecy slip out.

To his and Deanna's surprise, Iszarre seemed to ignore Eldrack's name. "Don't you see, Derek, I read my prophecy and assumed something truly terrible would happen. I focused all of my attention on what I thought would happen. I wasn't ready to use simple magic in a situation that might happen every day. I learned on that day that I should never let a prophecy dominate my vision. I also learned that the words of a prophecy can have many meanings."

Deanna had been thinking through the words of the prophecy. She couldn't remember all of them, but she had most memorized after reading it over and over. "Iszarre," she said, "I've been thinking about what the prophecy said, and I don't think that it could have a different meaning than what we are thinking."

Iszarre nodded and a slight smile crossed his face. "Deanna, did the prophecy use Eldrack's name?" he asked in a quiet voice.

"No, but it said the dark wizard," Deanna replied.

"Actually it said 'their sworn enemy' I think," Derek corrected.

"Oh, yeah, that's right," Deanna said.

"Well, you already have many friends," Iszarre said. "It is possible that you will gather more enemies along the way as well. You have twelve more moonstones to find. While you are doing that, you can ponder the meaning of 'sworn enemy.'"

Derek was about to say something, but Iszarre said, "Ah, I see Glabber's coming with a platter of dancing Yahoran melons, spicy waffles, and ice cold Vidolan goat milk. Delicious!"

# 2 Spur of the Moment

"Delicious," Deanna echoed as she wolfed down a forkful of spicy waffle dipped in sugar bush nectar. "Weird, but delicious."

"Huh?" Derek said as he tried to spear a piece of melon dancing across his plate.

"I was just saying," Deanna began, but she was interrupted by a loud clanking sound.

Somehow, they both knew what, or who, was making the noise. A moment later, Tobungus, the mushroom man, arrived at their table with the spurs on his cowboy boots clanking on the wooden floor boards.

"Howdy, Miss Deanna," he said with a smile, and tipped his hat to her.

"You are truly not of this world," Derek said.

"Oh no, Derek, you are not of this world," Tobungus corrected. "You see, I have this place in my blood."

"I didn't know you even had blood," a soft voice purred from the floor near Deanna. Zorell leapt onto a chair and shook his head at Tobungus.

"Ah, Tobungus, Zorell," Iszarre called out. "Everyone's here now. I have something for your journey to Tarook." He reached under the counter and grabbed what looked like a rusty chain with a glowing ball at the end before heading back to their table.

Derek and Deanna saw that he was holding something that looked like the locket that held the Book of Spells.

"Is that a spell book for Derek?" Deanna asked.

"Oh, this?" Iszarre replied. "No, no, this pendant is a workshop." He saw their confused looks and smiled. He touched a tiny button on the pendant, and a bell chimed faintly. "Gretz, can you come out?" he said to the pendant.

The pendant vibrated. A fountain of pink and purple light and sparks arched out and hit the floor. In the pool of light, a pair of feet appeared. Legs formed, and then a body, and finally a head. The man who stood before them was about three feet tall with a gray beard that shot out in all directions. He squinted through a monocle over his right eye, and he held a tattered tool box at his side.

"Deanna, Derek, I present Gretz, the Fixer," Izarre said happily.

"Hello," Deanna said a little nervously.

"I am most charmed to meet you, young lady," Gretz said. "Iszarre has told me all about you and your brother. It will be my great honor to help you in any way I can."

"Help us?" Derek asked.

"Why, of course," Iszarre replied. "Gretz putters around and fixes things."

"I do not putter," Gretz said sternly. "I fix broken magical connections."

"Yes, Master Gretz," Iszarre soothed. "I did not mean to insult you."

"What do you mean by magical connections?" Derek asked.

"Young Derek," Gretz began, "I know that you are new to this world, so you don't understand how magic really works yet. You probably still think that magic is just something that floats around and is used by wizards with a wand."

"Heh, heh," Gretz chuckled, shaking his shiny, bald head. "Magic is much more complicated than that. Magic comes in many different forms, and powerful wizards know how to use magic from a lot of sources at once. Here on Elestra, when magic comes up from the Ruby Core, it flows like a liquid through springs, streams, rivers, and oceans. It blows in the wind like a gas. It can even be a solid object."

"Actually, I kind of figured some of that out on our journeys so far," Derek said.

"Excellent," Gretz replied. "But, did you know that when you went through that arch in the Desert of the Crescent Dunes, tiny solid pieces of magic in the arch mixed with magic in the air to create that gateway?"

"No, I never thought about that," Derek said.

"Well, sometimes, these connections between different sources of magic are broken or weak," Gretz explained. "That's where I come in. I sense magical vibrations, and I can tell where magic is building up because a connection is broken. I fix those connections and get the magic flowing again."

Deanna spoke up for the first time. "How will we know if a magical connection is broken, if you're in your workshop?"

"Well, if you try to use a spell on an object, and it doesn't quite work right, then you might have a bad connection," Gretz said. "Or, if you're not sure, but you want to check things out, you can call me."

"I'm just afraid that we haven't been here long enough to know when magic isn't working like it should," Deanna replied.

"Well, you have your two friends to tell you if things seem out of place," Gretz said, pointing at

Zorell and Tobungus who were having a sword fight with long loaves of bread near the counter.

Before Deanna could say anything else, Gretz said, "I have a lot of work to do, so I have to get back, but don't hesitate to call me whenever you need me." He raised his hand to tip his hat, but realized that his head was bare. "I must have left my hat on the workbench," he said. "Well, anyway, I must be going." With a snap of his fingers, and a puff of smoke, he disappeared back into his workshop.

"Why don't you carry the workshop with you, so you can call Gretz out if a spell's not working right?" Derek said.

Deanna picked up the tiny workshop attached to the old chain and put it in her backpack.

Then, Deanna pulled out the Wand of Ondarell and walked over to Zorell and Tobungus and said, "Mind if I join in?"

As soon as the two rivals saw the wand, they dropped their bread and smiled guiltily. They both started to make up reasons that the fight was the other's fault, when Deanna raised her hand and said, "Stop, just stop."

"Okay, okay," Tobungus said, changing the subject. "What do you think of my new rootin' tootin' clothes?" He was proudly waving his hand up and down his cowboy outfit.

"Well, you have the boots, spurs, and hat," Deanna said.

"And, don't forget the lasso," Tobungus pointed out quickly.

"I'd say your outfit is complete," Derek added.

"Not quite," Tobungus began. "I have to stop by the used sock shop this morning." Seeing their empty plates and confused looks, he hurried toward the door. "Come on, I'll tell you all about it on the way."

Derek and Deanna shouted a quick "goodbye" to Iszarre, grabbed their backpacks, and scrambled out of their chairs to catch Tobungus who was now rushing out the door.

"Hey, wait up," Derek called out.

Once in the street, Tobungus explained, "Sometimes, I forget that you don't know everything about magic yet. Soon, you will understand that used socks are an important part of any wizard's supplies."

"I think Deanna is doing quite well without chasing after smelly, sweaty socks," Zorell hissed.

"Ignore the flea trap," Tobungus said quickly. "Magic doesn't just happen. Well, actually, it does. Hoo boy, this is complicated.

Okay, each person has a different ability or capacity to use magic. Yours is obviously extremely high, as we have seen. That does not mean that you always have the same level of magic within you. The air and water in Elestra have traces of magic. The foods you eat have even more. Certain items that you use, such as your wand, channel magic into you."

"But, that doesn't explain dirty socks," Deanna said, trying to keep up.

"Right, right," Tobungus said. "But, as you use magic, you have to get rid of it. Then there's the excess magic that builds up while you sleep. Here's where socks come in. All that used or extra magic sinks to your feet because it is so heavy. When your feet sweat, the waste magic drains away."

"You're joking, right?" Derek laughed.

"If it's waste magic, why would we want it?" Deanna asked.

"I never joke about used socks, Derek." Tobungus turned to Deanna and said, "Most of it is extra magic. Even the used magic can be used differently by different people. The feet are really quite remarkable. They can soak up magic as well as they can sweat it away. By wearing someone else's socks, you can get a magical boost."

"I don't mean to sound skeptical," Derek

said, "but we haven't used any used socks yet, and we've done just fine."

"Yes, Derek," Tobungus said, "but I heard you mention Tarook."

Zorell stopped in his tracks and his eyes grew wide. "What is it, Zorell?" Deanna asked.

"For once, King Compost is right. We'd better get some extra supplies," Zorell said just above a whisper.

After three more blocks, Tobungus led the group down a stairway and into a dimly lit shop. The crowded shop was eerily silent. Tobungus waited a few seconds and then rang a bell on the counter. After a minute or two, a tiny man with a patch over his left eye stepped out from behind a set of shelves. He had a sock-shaped patch on his shirt that said, 'Zum.'

"Ah, Tobungus," he said, "what can I do for you?"

"We need, oh, let's say, eight pairs of socks. Make sure they're level five or higher," Tobungus said. The little man nodded and slipped into the back room. Tobungus explained to Derek and Deanna that the level of the socks was determined by the strength of magic in them. Level fives would give them a nice boost.

When the old man returned, his patch was

over his right eye. "I'm afraid that I only have two pairs of level fives. The rest are threes," he said.

"I see he's dealt with you before," Zorell said to Tobungus. "Excuse me sir," the cat purred, "but do you know who this young lady is?"

The old man squinted at her with his left eye and shrugged.

"She is the great wizard who brought light back to Amemnop. She has defeated Eldrack on three separate occasions," Zorell explained.

The old man moved the patch from his eye to his left ear. "Oh, dear me. I'm so sorry that I didn't recognize you. I'll go back and see if I have anything that I might have missed."

A minute later, the old man returned with a dark wooden barrel. Derek noticed that the patch was now covering his right ear. "I don't know how I missed this," he said nervously. "I have ten sets of socks worn by the great wizard Glorat. The socks have been aging in Thesallian cormac wood barrels in the Moonlight Forest for twenty years. They should be at least level eight. Let me get my Magalyzer to test them." He scurried off to the back room again.

When he returned, he had the patch over his nose. "Ah, yes," he said in a whiny voice that sounded like his nose was being pinched, "nine pairs are level eight and one is level nine. Very nice." Before anyone could say anything, he ran to take his Mag-alyzer back to its hiding place.

"We'll give you sixty gold dracamas," Tobungus called back.

"Mmm, mmm," the man mumbled.

Derek saw that the old man now had the patch over his mouth. "Oh, this is ridiculous," he said. He reached out and pulled the patch away from the old man's mouth.

"Why, thank you, young man," the shopkeeper said. "That pesky patch has a mind of its own."

"Now then," Derek asked, "how does sixty dracamas sound?"

"Well," the man said slowly.

"We'll make it seventy, if you promise to keep this sale a secret," Zorell hissed.

"Seventy," the man said in surprise. "Of course, the sale is just between us." He scooped up the seventy gold coins and handed the barrel to Derek.

With the old socks stuffed into Derek's backpack, they left the store and headed back into the bright morning sunlight. Tobungus started clanking along the street as fast as he could, but Deanna stood still, looking toward Zorell.

"Maybe you'd better explain that bit about keeping the sale a secret," Deanna said, feeling as if Zorell was worried about something.

"Very well," Zorell purred. "If an enemy wizard knows what type of magic you're using to boost your power, he can choose attacks which will be more effective against you." Looking at Tobungus, he said, "You forgot to mention that, didn't you squish head."

# 3  Don't Get Carried Away

"Whoa," Deanna said.  "So, there's a chance that these great sweaty socks that you just had to have could actually help Eldrack?"

"No, no, absolutely not," Tobungus stammered.  "Okay, yes.  But only if he knows the precise type of magic that the socks hold."

"Do you mean offensive or defensive magic?" Deanna asked.

"No," Tobungus said confidently.  "There are many types of magic, such as ice magic, fire magic, and water magic.  There are at least thirty or forty types of magic."

"That is certainly true," Zorell purred.  "But, most wizards use ice, fire, water, or wind magic.  The other types are much less common."

"So, what type of magic did the wizard who wore our socks use?" Deanna asked.

"Glorat was known as an ice wizard," Zorell explained.  "If you use an ice spell with the socks, it will be much more powerful."

"Since Glorat was famous for using ice spells, couldn't Eldrack guess that's the type of magic that the socks contained?" Derek added.

"Well, yes," Tobungus said sheepishly. "But, even Zorell agreed that the socks might be useful on this journey." Derek didn't look convinced. "Trust me. Eldrack won't find out. I've known the man who runs the shop for a long time."

"What was his name again?" Deanna asked.

"Whose name?" Tobungus asked.

"The man who ran the sock shop," Deanna replied.

"Ah, yes, his name was Gretz," Tobungus answered.

"No, Tobungus," Deanna said. "Gretz is the fixer who lives in the workshop on the chain in my backpack. Try again."

"Oh, yes, that's right," Tobungus said softly. "The shop owner's name was Zippy."

"Wrong again," Deanna snapped.

"Herkimer del Stimpkin," Tobungus guessed.

"His name was Zum," Deanna said seriously.

"You must remember that I am terrible with names," Tobungus said. "Now that you say it, I know that his name is Zum. Oh, the stories I could tell you about Zum."

Derek cut in, "Look, Deanna, we'll treat the socks as a last resort. Let's get to the Library and figure out what we need to do.  We'll just prepare like normal."

The walk to the Library was quiet.  Everyone was wrapped up in their own thoughts.  Tobungus tried to think of a clever insult to even the score with Zorell, but all he could think was that Zorell had made him look stupid without using clever names. *What a depressing thought*, he sighed.

The Library was becoming a familiar haven where they felt safe while researching the mysteries of Elestra.  At the start and end of each adventure, they found themselves at the Library learning more about Elestra's wonders.  They found that the more they learned, the more they still needed to learn.

The book fairies were excited to see them arrive, because they always requested large stacks of books on topics that were important to the entire kingdom.  The fairies felt like they were helping in the twins' fight against Eldrack.

"We need anything you have on Tarook or the Pillars of Tarook," Deanna said to the head librarian.  Before the librarian could clap her hands, a swarm of tiny book fairies zipped down from their perches, awaiting instructions.  Some zoomed high into the bookshelves that reached to the ceiling several stories above.  Others maneuvered through gaps in books to get to the back of the library, lifting layers of dust with their fluttering wings.

Within minutes, a stack of books taller than Derek stood on their table. Deanna and Derek each chose promising titles to begin their search. "Listen to this," Deanna began, "Tarook was an artist of some sort. This book says that he used magic to bring his art to life. He designed temples, drew landscapes, and wrote songs, and then used his magic to make them parts of the real world."

Derek looked over at Tobungus who was tipping his cowboy hat to one of the book fairies. "I hardly think that real world describes this place," he said, shaking his head. "Anyway, how did he make music part of the real world?"

"I'm not sure," Deanna said. "It seems that there is a valley where his music floats on the air to highlight the natural beauty of the surroundings. He sounds interesting, but I'm not sure what he has to do with moonstones."

"I might be able to help with that," Derek said. "I picked up a book called *The Late Works of Tarook,* and it looks like his last project was supposed to be his masterpiece. He was visited by a great ice wizard named Glorat." Derek stopped for a second. "I'm terrible with names. Where do I know that name, Glorat?" Derek asked teasingly.

"The socks belonged to Glorat," Zorell

purred. "And, you may recall that if Eldrack knows the type of magic the socks contain, he will be able to use that against us."

"I'm telling you, Eldrack won't find out that the socks belonged to Glorat," Tobungus said between clenched teeth.

"Look, guys," Deanna said, "We'll just have to outsmart Eldrack. We'll use other types of magic before we use the socks, and then we'll switch over to ice spells. That should keep Eldrack from knowing what we're planning with the socks."

Derek looked over at Tobungus who had a dark look on his face. Something was clearly bothering him, but Derek continued, "Glorat asked Tarook to design a great temple where a treasure would be hidden. Tarook disappeared soon after designing the building. Listen to this:

"Glorat searched for the great artist. He ventured all over Elestra until he found a clue suggesting that Tarook's Temple had appeared in the ice fields of Mount Drasius. Glorat also found Tarook's design, which included seven great pillars filled with a rainbow of magic.

When Glorat reached the temple, he found that Tarook had failed to finish his final work. There were no pillars. Any treasure that the *temple held was probably lost forever.*

"Well, it sounds like we know where we're going," Deanna said.

"Yes," Zorell purred, "Mount Drasius." He saw Derek and Deanna watching his pleasure at the prospect of going to this new destination. "Felius, the patron wizard of my species, was born on Mount Drasius. My species enjoys strong magical protection there."

Derek and Deanna led Tobungus and Zorell outside, satisfied that they had figured out where they needed to go. The sun was bright and warm. Deanna breathed in the sweet air and said, "Now this is a perfect day."

Before Zorell could say anything, a pair of massive talons grabbed him and lifted him into the air. Derek and Deanna saw that the talons belonged to a huge hawk-like bird that was rising quickly out of sight. Tobungus looked worried at first, and then a huge smile crept across his squishy cheeks. He knew that the chance of a lifetime was upon him.

Deanna reached for the Wand of Ondarell, as Tobungus put his plan into action. He had his lasso out and was able to get it around the neck of another huge bird which appeared to be following the bird that had snatched Zorell. He swung himself up onto the back of the bird and used the rope around its neck to steer it.

Tobungus swooped down and picked up Derek and Deanna. "These are jellybirds," he said. "Don't think about using magic on the one carrying Zorell, or it will drop him. It's pretty high already, so that's not a good idea."

Deanna was about to suggest that she could catch Zorell with a magical spell, but Tobungus cut her off, "Just leave it to me."

Tobungus kicked his spurs into the side of the bird to make it fly faster. It seemed to work, as the wind whipped their hair more and more. The jellybird carrying Zorell didn't seem to notice that it was being chased, so it made no attempts to lose the second bird.

The first jellybird led them past the peak of a steep mountain and over a thick forest. It reached an opening where the kids could see dozens of nests, the size of cars, dotting the land. The bird dropped Zorell into one of the nests and circled around the stunned cat. Before he could run, the jellybird opened its mouth.

Deanna was afraid that the bird was getting ready to eat Zorell. She raised her wand, even though they were still a long way off. "No," Tobungus called out. "This is the best part," he whispered.

"Listen, Tobungus, you may hate each other, but I can't believe that you would let Zorell get eaten by that bird," Deanna shouted.

"He's not going to be eaten, Deanna," Tobungus said. "Jellybirds don't eat cats. Just watch. Trust me," he added.

Deanna held her breath, hoping that Tobungus was telling the truth. She watched as the massive bird lowered its beak and swallowed the stunned cat, as Tobungus sat laughing next to her.

# 4 Sticky Situation

"Tobungus!" Deanna shouted. "How could you do this?" She jumped off of their jellybird, which had landed in an area that was filled with dozens of other jellybirds wandering through a maze of giant nests.

"What?" Tobungus choked out between fits of laughter.

"Do you really have the nerve to ask why I'm so upset?" Deanna screeched. "You tricked me into letting that bird eat Zorell."

"Deanna," Tobungus said, seeing that she was serious, "I told you that the jellybird would not eat Zorell, and I was telling the truth. There, look for yourself," he said, pointing to the huge nest.

Sure enough, the bird had not eaten Zorell. Instead, it seemed to be gagging on the furry morsel. After a minute or so, it spit out a thick jelly cocoon containing the cat. Zorell was covered so thickly that he couldn't move. Deanna looked at Tobungus, waiting for an explanation.

"Just wait a bit longer," Tobungus

whispered, still shaking with laughter.

A few seconds later, the huge jellybird took off and flew back toward Amemnop.    "Okay, now he's going to try to find another person or animal to act as a core for another mound of jelly."

Tobungus saw that Deanna looked confused, so he explained, "Jellybirds eat only honey made by thunder bees.  These thunder bees can't get nectar from plants because when they land, the flowers close up in fear of the loud thunder produced by a thunder bee swarm.  The jellybirds create a sweet liquid like nectar by sniffing the flowers of the Fodulius Forest.  They swallow small animals and creatures such as pixies and fairies, and spit them back out covered in the jelly.  The thunder bees go to the jellied animal and eat the jelly.  They use it to make their honey, which the jellybirds then eat."

"Talk about a weird food web," Derek laughed, thinking back to a science class he had the year before.

"Huh?" Tobungus muttered.

"Never mind," Derek replied.

"So, we're supposed to let Zorell sit in that goo until the bees eat it off of him?" Deanna asked.

"No, Deanna," Tobungus said, "Now, it's time to use your wand."

Deanna pulled the Wand of Ondarell from

her belt. She thought through the spells she had mastered. She wondered which type of spell would work best. Should she burn the jelly off, hit it with a wave of water, or simply try to make it disappear?

Meanwhile, Tobungus pulled a small ball that looked like a marble from his pocket. "I have to save a picture of this," he said. He threw the marble at Zorell, and a few seconds later, it bounced back into his hands. "It's a picture ball," he said. The tiny ball captured a picture of Zorell covered in jelly, so that Tobungus could see his foe in this embarrassing position whenever he wanted.

Derek interrupted her thinking. "Deanna," he whispered, "we're not alone." He pulled her down behind some bushes and pointed ahead.

She looked in the direction he was pointing. All she saw, other than the flock of jellybirds, was a bunch of boulders, but she couldn't see anyone hiding behind them. "Where?" she asked. "Is someone behind one of those rocks?"

"No," Derek whispered. "It's the rocks I'm worried about." He saw her confusion. "Just look," he said.

She turned back to the boulders and saw one of them creep forward a bit. Then another followed. She scanned the entire group and finally saw one open a pair of eyes on its rocky face. She gasped and stumbled backward. Before she could catch her breath, a familiar form in a dark cape stepped from behind the largest of the rocky creatures.

"Oh, no," Derek said. "Deanna, you better come up with something good. We're pretty far away from Amemnop."

"I have an idea," Tobungus said. Turning to Deanna, he whispered, "Use your wand to cut a small hole in Zorell's jelly cocoon." Before she could ask why, he said, "I'll be right back." He slipped out of sight behind a stand of bushes.

Deanna crouched down and leveled the wand in Zorell's direction. She whispered a few words which Derek couldn't hear and a thin thread of light shot from the wand. One end of Zorell's cocoon started to glow, and soon they could see their friend's head, even though he was still trapped.

"Deanna," a loud voice boomed, "Come out, and we can talk."

"That's original," Deanna shouted back from her hiding place.

"I give you my word that I only want to talk to you," Eldrack said, softening his tone.

"Yeah, well, you see, I don't really trust the word of a dark wizard who kidnapped my grandfather, and his father, and well, his father, and oh gee, his father, too. You get the picture," Deanna said. "It's just one of those rules I try to live by. I'm sure you understand."

"Oh, Deanna," Eldrack said, but he got no further. A huge jellybird swooped in and picked up Zorell. Tobungus was riding on the bird's back and guiding it with his lasso and spurs. He swung around by Derek and Deanna and pulled on the reins. The bird squeezed its talons tighter on Zorell's cocoon. The pressure pushed Zorell out into the waiting arms of Deanna.

"I'll be right back," Tobungus said again. He guided the bird toward Eldrack and dug his spurs into the beast's side. The shock made the bird loosen its grip on the jelly cocoon which landed on Eldrack. Tobungus shot back around and picked up Derek, Deanna, and Zorell.

Eldrack was quickly dissolving the jelly with a spell that Deanna had never seen. "We'd better go quickly," Tobungus said. "Eldrack can hop on one of these birds too, and then it will be a race to safety."

"Now, I have an idea," Deanna said. She pointed the wand at the ground near Eldrack, and said, "*Seismio terrumpto!*" The ground began to vibrate. The boulders near Eldrack started to bounce and roll around as the land was shaken by the earthquake. Eldrack was swept off of his feet and had to use every ounce of his strength to avoid being crushed.

Tobungus guided the bird low over the forest and into a rolling fog that was rising from a lake in front of them. "This fog should hide us pretty well," he said.

The jellybird flew across the lake and into a narrow canyon. It zipped between thin, towering hills covered with grass on its way to the canyon's far side.

Deanna looked back to see if Eldrack was following them. She couldn't see any other large birds anywhere in her field of view. She was feeling better about their chances of avoiding Eldrack before getting to Mt. Drasius.

The jellybird shot out of the canyon and flew along a river that cut through a lush meadow. Hundreds of bright orange animals that looked like six-legged horses ran below them, shouting happily to the jellybird and its passengers.

"Deanna," Tobungus shouted over the whipping wind.

"What's wrong, Tobungus?" she yelled back.

"Do you have a spell to keep us dry?" he replied. "We're going to head over that large lake up ahead and it looks like it's raining."

"No problem," Deanna said. "I'll use the *Umbrellius* spell when we get closer." She had the wand ready to cast the spell as soon as they felt the first raindrops.

"I hope that one of you knows how to get to Mount Drasius from here," Derek said. "We're pretty far from Amemnop, and I wasn't paying attention to the route the jellybird took to get here."

"It doesn't get any easier from here," Zorell hissed, as he licked globs of jelly from his fur. "Mount Drasius is in the middle of the Galloran Barrens. It is a region with nothing—no plants, no animals, no water, not even any deserts. It's just rock."

"Volcanic rock," Tobungus added cheerfully.

Derek checked that their packs were secure. "It's a good thing we picked up food from Glabber for the trip," he said.

"Yes." Zorell continued, "As I said before I was interrupted, Mount Drasius sits in the middle of the Barrens. It is a volcano that only erupts from one side." He rolled his tongue against his teeth as a bit of jelly and fur stuck in his mouth. "The interesting thing is that the mountain rotates, so the eruptions have covered the entire area with lava that has cooled to black rock, but has not been covered with soil yet. The other side of the mountain is covered in snow and ice."

"I thought you said your species was from there," Deanna said quickly.

"Well, we're not actually from there. We all go there during our lives. There are strips of lush jungles between the ice fields and the volcanic flows. It's a paradise for many species," Zorell purred.

"But we're going to the ice fields," Tobungus said happily.

"Why are you so happy about visiting a glacier?" Derek asked suspiciously.

Tobungus looked at Zorell, filled with joy at having the cat owe him his life. He did not answer Derek, instead aiming his words at Zorell, "I saved our little kitty's life." He sighed contentedly.

# 5 Sounds Like Fun, or Maybe Not

Tobungus' happiness was equal only to Zorell's sadness. *How could he have let himself get into a situation where Tobungus had to save him?* He knew that he could not insult Tobungus as long as he owed his rival his life.

He briefly thought about running away, but he could not abandon Deanna and Derek. He believed in their cause too strongly. He had to figure out a way to deal with Tobungus' gloating, *but how?* Then, it hit him. He smiled and breathed a deep breath of freedom. He would right this wrong and was sure that he would get his chance on Mt. Drasius.

"Why do you look so happy?" Tobungus asked. He wanted Zorell to squirm.

"I'm just happy to be alive, thanks to you, Tobungus," Zorell said while trying to keep from laughing.

"Well, I couldn't have the family pet stung by the big bad bees. We might run into a mouse that needs catching, after all," Tobungus replied.

"Just show me the mouse, and I'll be glad to

catch it for you," Zorell said quickly.

Derek looked suspiciously at Zorell and Tobungus. He had never seen them be nice to each other before. He didn't realize that in Elestra, when someone's life is saved from certain perils, including a jellybird attack, Valuvian toe itch, or a weeklong hug from a marmat serpent, they owe their life to their rescuer. Insults or physical attacks against their rescuer disrupt the magical flow and lead to nightmares about bathing in bubbling pots of skunkfish blubber while tiny bugs sing horribly off key opera songs.

Deanna didn't have the patience to figure out what Tobungus and Zorell were up to. "Excuse me," she said, "but how do we get to the Galloran Barrens? Do either of you know?"

"Of course," Tobungus answered. "After we cross this lake, we'll head up to the top of Mount Boolia. It should only take an hour or so. When we get there, we can ride the slingline to the Barrens."

"I don't think I like the sound of a sling line," Derek muttered.

"Oh, it's fun, really," Zorell said. "The idea is simple. It's like a, well, a big elastic rope. Do you know what I mean?"

"Like a big rubber band?" Derek replied.

"Yes, that sounds about right," Zorell said.

"At the end of the line is a large ball. Riders get inside the ball. The line is then shot at a target location. There are many of them around sling line launch stations. When the sling line stretches out and the ball reaches its destination, a huge hook grabs the ball. The sling line releases and snaps back to the starting point."

"How far from Mount Boolia is the Barrens station?" Deanna asked.

"In terms you would understand," Zorell said, thinking furiously, "it's about three hundred miles."

"What kind of magic do they use to get the line to go fast enough so that it doesn't just fall to the ground?" Deanna asked.

"They don't use magic," Tobungus said, "at least for the traveling part. Magic is used to keep riders in place."

"Oh, no," Derek whispered.

Deanna looked confused, but Zorell said knowingly, "I see that you have figured out why it's called a sling line, Derek."

Derek turned to his sister. "They don't use magic. They use physics," he began. "My guess, Deanna, is that the line is tight at first. They start swinging it in a circle around the launcher. As it picks up speed, they release more of the sling line.

It has to keep getting faster so that the ball doesn't hit the ground. It sounds like we'll be zipping around the mountain on a huge rubber band, going faster and faster, until the ball we're riding in is grabbed by a mechanical hand."

"It sounds like an amusement park ride," Deanna said. "Only faster, and hopefully the lines will be shorter."

"That's what worries me," Derek said. "It always seems that half the rides at the amusement park are broken down. I'd rather not have that happen while we're riding."

"Well, then, it seems that we should call Gretz out when we get to the sling line station," Deanna said. "Maybe he can check everything out for us."

"That's a great idea," Derek replied.

Everyone settled in for the hour flight to the Mount Boolia sling line station. Tobungus marveled at Zorell's ability to tolerate their new relationship. Zorell struggled to imagine when his plan would begin to unfold. Derek tried to guess the speeds that the sling line would travel, and Deanna ran through every spell she could remember to plan a way to slow the sling line ball down if necessary.

They arrived at the sling line station and saw

a purple ball with six seats inside. It was attached to a sling line that was no more than an inch thick. A four-legged man with six arms scurried out from a control hut with a clipboard in one of his hands. "May I help you?" he asked politely.

"Yes," Tobungus answered. "We need passage to the Galloran Barrens. Just the four of us."

"Very well," the man said. "I have to ask you some questions first, to make sure that the ride will be safe for you."

"Sure," Deanna said, wondering what types of safety issues they would face.

"Okay," the man said. "Do you all have a heart, lungs, stomach, kidneys, multiple eyes, and a brain?"

"Yes," Derek laughed.

"And are all of these organs working properly?" the man continued.

Zorell wanted to make a comment about Tobungus' brain, but held his tongue. "Yes," he purred, "everything is in working order."

"Excellent," the man said. "In the past six hours, have any of you eaten sour purple food, been bitten by a sponge beetle, gotten a toe massage from Nootoran slugs, argued with a shrieking pixie, or suffered a level seven magical attack?"

"No," Deanna answered, wondering what any of those things had to do with riding the sling line.

"Well, then, I guess we're ready," the man said. "Please have a seat in the passenger compartment and I'll get you going."

"If you don't mind," Deanna said, "we'd like to have a friend make sure everything's safe for us."

"Of course," the man said. "But, I don't see anyone else here."

"He's in my backpack," Deanna said.

"Ah, very well," the man said, with no hint of surprise.

Deanna reached into her backpack and pulled out the rusty chain with the glowing ball that contained Gretz's workshop. She knocked on the ball and called, "Gretz, can you come out and help us?"

With a flash and a fizzing sound, Gretz popped out of the ball and grew to his normal size. "Ah, Ms. Deanna," the Fixer said happily. "How can I help you?"

"We're about to ride a slingline," Deanna said, waving to the station around them.

"And, you see," Derek added, "we're not entirely sure that everything's in good shape. We'd hate to have the slingline break down when we're halfway to our destination."

"Ah, yes, that would be unfortunate," Gretz said. "All sorts of bouncing and flipping, and what not."

"Yes, and what not," Deanna repeated. "Do you think you can check things out for us?"

"Well, you see, the slingline is mostly mechanical, and not magical," Gretz explained. "However, there are permanent magic spells that protect the slingline machinery. I can certainly check those for you."

"That would be great," Deanna said, stepping out of the way.

Gretz walked around the room, blowing a whistle at various pieces of equipment. More than once, he dug his finger in his ear and said, "Wow, that whistle's loud."

"Well?" Deanna prodded. "Is everything okay?"

"Oh, yes," Gretz replied. "The protective spells are much stronger than I expected. In fact, I've never seen such strong protections before. I'd say you'll be safe on your trip."

"Thanks, Gretz," Deanna said.

"You're quite welcome," he replied. He did a little dance and slowly shrunk down to the size of a pea and scurried into his workshop ball.

"Well, then, let's get on board," Deanna said happily.

"You seem ready to go," Derek replied.

"Oh, don't think that the wand will be anywhere but in my hand, ready to use a spell to bring the ball gently to the ground," she said.

They climbed into the cramped ball and found the seats heavily padded and comfortable. "Please keep your arms in the car at all times," Derek whispered to Deanna, hoping that riding the sling line would be like riding a roller coaster. He quickly discovered that no roller coaster he had ever been on prepared him for this.

The six armed man used all of his arms in a blinding flurry of activity on the controls in his control hut. The launcher began to rotate, and the ball swung quickly in a complete circle. Slowly at first, the sling line was let out, so their distance from the launcher inched upward. As they got used to the rotation, the ball accelerated. They moved further from the station.

Derek understood why they had to pick up speed. He tried to yell over the whipping wind, but he didn't know if Deanna could hear him. "If we don't speed up, the sling line will fall to the ground. It's going to get a lot faster than this."

If Deanna heard him, she didn't show it. She

clutched the wand in one hand with her eyes frozen in a terrified stare.

# 6  Drumbeats and Snowballs

*Faster, faster, too fast, way too fast.  Help!*
Deanna was fighting a wave of fear caused by the
still accelerating sling line ball.  She struggled to
turn her head slightly to check the others.  Derek
looked as scared as she did.  Zorell's whiskers were
swept back by the wind.  His cheeks were pulled
back in a bizarre smile that had nothing to do with
happiness.  Tobungus had fallen asleep.  His mouth
hung open, and his snoring was loud enough to be
heard over the whipping wind.

As quickly as the ride started, it was over.
There was no lurching motion as the ball stopped.
They just stopped.  A voice called out from
somewhere behind them, "Sit back and breathe
deeply for a few minutes."

"There's great, there's good, there's bad, and
then there's a sling line ride," Derek whispered.

After her head cleared, Deanna elbowed
Tobungus hard enough to wake him up from his
deep sleep.  Before Tobungus could ask why she
had been so rough, everyone in the group heard a

noise that seemed out of place.

It sounded like drums, but the beats thumped very far away. It wasn't even really a sound, but more like the ghost of a sound. When the wind blew harder, they lost it, only to hear whispers of the drum beat again when the wind calmed.

"What is that?" Derek asked softly, as if he had to whisper to avoid detection, even though no one was around, other than the man working the controls on this end of the sling line ride.

"Why didn't I bring them?" Tobungus grimaced.

"Bring what?" Deanna asked.

"My bagpipes," Tobungus sighed. Deanna simply stared at him.

"Guardian Deanna," Zorell purred, "I believe that Tobungus thinks that the sound is most likely from the drummers of the Lost Army of Light."

"Is that one of those magical armies we heard about before?" Derek asked.

"In a way," Zorell answered. "The Lost Army of Light is something of a myth. No one knows for sure if it exists."

"Oh, it exists!" Tobungus said seriously. "Don't listen to the skeptic."

"Not everyone agrees with that," Zorell said.

"The Lost Army of Light was not involved in the last magical tournament, and there is no record of their participation in any tournament before that. Some believe that the Lost Army of Light is the ultimate magical army. It is a force that exists in the mists of time and only shows itself when the true ruler of Elestra needs its help."

"If that's true, it could mean that Eldrack is gaining more power than we know. The king may be in trouble," Deanna murmured.

"That is possible," Zorell hissed. "Tobungus thinks that hearing the advancing drum line of the Army of Light means that the magical warriors have chosen to be near you and Derek. If he's right, that would mean that they have determined that your mission is crucial for the true king's survival."

"But why the bagpipes?" Derek whispered to Zorell, without needing to keep his voice down— Tobungus was furiously scanning the horizon for any sign of a magical army massing.

"I'm certain that you two have noticed that Tobungus likes to, oh, how do I say it? Well, he likes to make himself a part of every situation. He wants to connect with the Lost Army of Light by playing his bagpipes with the magical drummers."

Derek couldn't believe that Tobungus would think that playing bagpipes would connect him to a mythical army of magical warriors. "Yo, Tobungus, what's with the bagpipes?"

"Ah, Derek, I'm glad you asked," Tobungus grinned. "Have you ever witnessed the glory of a bagpipe duel?"

Derek's jaw dropped. "A bagpipe. . . duel?"

"Aye, Derek," Tobungus said with a fake Scottish accent, which Derek couldn't understand since Scotland had no connection to Elestra. "Captain Kitty Litter over there may be right that the drums are from the Lost Army of Light, but it is also possible that Eldrack has raised one or more armies and has gotten bold enough to allow them to play their marching songs. What he forgot to mention was that my bagpipes are more than a musical instrument. But, you will have to wait until we return to Amemnop to learn more."

Derek was about to protest, but Zorell cut in, "Whether the drums are from an army shadowing your moves for protection or from Eldrack's army, it is clear that we should move quickly to retrieve the next moonstone." The quartet agreed, and they headed through the lush jungle strip toward the ice fields on the non-volcanic side of Mount Drasius.

The jungle was warm, but a gentle breeze brushed their faces. They heard the songs of birds high in the trees all around them. The sounds of animals rushing through the underbrush startled them at first, but when they realized that nothing jumped out at them, they were able to enjoy being so close to unseen creatures.

The jungle was a place where everyone in the group was comfortable. Zorell loved the warmth and the jungle's connection to his people. Tobungus loved the humidity which reminded him of resting on warm, moist moss. Derek and Deanna were amazed by the sights and sounds, as well as the beautiful smells from the huge flowers that appeared all around them.

The only difficult part of the jungle was when the path was blocked by a huge tree. The path was steep in this area, and they were worried about climbing around the tree to move onward.

"Oh man!" Derek said. "We need to find a way around this tree."

"Oh, pardon me," the tree said. "I got distracted by a patch of rare hooga flowers. I'll move aside so you can pass."

The tree struggled out of the ground and walked on its roots to a spot up the mountain next to the path where it dug its roots back in. "Have a nice hike," the tree shouted back down to the group.

"Thank you," Deanna called back. She hopped over the shallow hole where the tree's roots had been and led the others further along the path.

The rest of the hike seemed almost as normal as a hike in the woods back home to Derek and Deanna. None of the plants talked to them, and the only sound they heard besides the singing birds was Tobungus panting as he struggled to keep up.

After another twenty minutes of hiking, they saw a sign that announced that the border of the Realm of Ice was five minutes ahead. As they passed the sign, it said, "Ahem. I see that you are heading to the glorious Ice Lands. Are you prepared for the majestic coldness that you will experience?"

"How cold are you talking?" Derek asked.

"Heh, heh, heh," the sign chuckled. "Young man, you may think that you know cold, but there are places in the Ice Lands where ice freezes a second time. Of course, those places are far from the border. There is even a legend of a place that is so cold that it freezes magic itself. The lands you will cross into are very cold, but they are not that cold."

"We'll use our magic to provide protection from the cold," Deanna said, showing the sign the Wand of Ondarell.

"Very well," the sign replied. "Have a glorious adventure in the coldest and coolest magical realm in Elestra."

The final minutes of hiking through the jungle were peaceful and warm. Everything changed the second they crossed into the ice fields. The wind went from a warm breeze to a wickedly cold blast. The humidity was replaced by blowing snow.

Deanna used the wand to whip up magical capes to keep them warm, and all seemed fine, until a snowball flew from the blowing snow and pelted Derek on the cheek. Before they could react, a barrage of snowballs rained down upon them. Deanna's first thought was that snowballs were an odd choice for Eldrack's henchmen.

A white shape hopped out of the snow and then back in before anyone could see what it was. They all had their hands over their faces to block the next wave of snowballs, but Derek thought that he saw a thick tail on one of the white creatures. Tobungus, who usually seemed to know every creature in Elestra, was at a loss.

Another shape flitted in front of Derek. "I don't believe what I just saw," he said.

"What is it?" Deanna asked nervously.

"It looked like a kangaroo," Derek answered, "only all white. And it looked like it was pulling a snowball from its pouch."

"Well, let's see how they like it if we melt their snow," Deanna said as she raised the wand.

"No, Deanna," Zorell shouted. "There are hundreds of these snowhoppers. You'll never be able to melt enough snow to stop them."

"Then what should we do?" Deanna asked desperately.

"They want to have a snowball fight," Zorell hissed. "I suggest that you start throwing snowballs now."

Derek and Tobungus dove to the ground and packed snowballs to throw at the odd snow kangaroos. For every snowball they threw, twenty more flew back at them. Even though they were being hit more often than they could throw snowballs, they were laughing hysterically.

"This is ridiculous," Deanna laughed. Suddenly, she realized that even if she couldn't melt the snow, she could use the wand. She swept the wand around and a loop of snowballs like a giant string of pearls rose into the air and flew at the creatures.

Deanna spun in a circle like a figure skater, whipping her storm of snowballs faster and faster. After what seemed like an hour, a squeaky, but loud voice yelled, "Enough!"

The largest of the snow kangaroos hopped

out of the blizzard that had been kicked up by the unending rain of snowballs. "My name is Boldorf, son of Krendar. I am the current Leader of the Drasian Snowhoppers. We thank you for an excellent snowball fight," he said.

Hundreds of other voices yipped with joy. "Never has an outsider been able to deliver so many snowballs," Boldorf called out. "In our hearts and minds, you are all honorary snowhoppers. But," he added slowly, "why have you come to the ice fields?"

"We have come on a mission in the name of King Barado," Deanna began, waving her hand which still held the Wand of Ondarell.

"The great wand," Boldorf exclaimed. "Look, my snowhoppers, she holds the wand that our great Tarook described."

"Tarook was a . . . ," Derek began.

"A snowhopper," Boldorf finished for him proudly. "Yes, he was our great artist and wizard. But many years ago, he disappeared. Our people searched endlessly, but we never found any sign of him."

Derek and Deanna looked at each other, thinking that this story sounded like the disappearances of their ancestors. "What did you mean about Tarook describing this wand?" Deanna asked.

"The Great Tarook's final work was the Temple of Ice. There is a carving on one of the walls showing this wand," Boldorf explained. "Now let me ask you, are you searching for the Temple of Ice?"

Deanna looked at the others, and then back to Boldorf. "Yes, I believe we are," she answered.

"Come my snowhoppers," Boldorf roared, "we are leaving to show our new friends to the Temple." Without warning, hundreds of wildly excited snowhoppers hopped out of the storm and led the group up the mountain toward the low hanging snow clouds near the summit.

# 7 The Light Within

About halfway up the mountain, Boldorf took a moment to talk to Deanna. "I don't mean to be rude," he began, "but may I ask why you wish to go to the Temple? I know that you come in the name of the King and you possess the great wand, so you must be very powerful, but we have searched the Temple time and again, and we have never found anything other than the murals and statues that tell our history."

"I'm never exactly sure why we have to go to the places where we are sent," Deanna explained honestly. "I'm hoping that we can find information that will help us defeat the dark wizard Eldrack."

"Eldrack, here?" Boldorf said in a voice that sounded more like a hiss than the usual, happy yipping of a snowhopper.

"I'm afraid so," Deanna said. "We're in a race against Eldrack and his armies to find magical items that will be important when the next magical tournament starts."

"The tournament nears," Boldorf muttered. "One of our legends tells that there will be no tournament."

"No tournament?" Deanna said in a shocked voice. "But, the armies will be gathering soon."

"Yes, the armies will gather, but not for a tournament," Boldorf said. "Instead, they will fight a great battle. The greatest battle that Elestra has ever seen." He saw Deanna's worried look. "At least, that's what the legend says. But, then again, we have legends that say a lot of crazy things."

Deanna's look grew more serious. "The problem is that the legend doesn't sound that crazy."

"Then, I can pledge our support to your cause," Boldorf said proudly, "but I must warn you that we cannot take too much time at the Temple. The volcano on the far side grows restless. Before long, it will erupt again. When it does, the ice fields will shake with fear before the protection of the patron wizards calms the boiling heart of Mount Drasius."

Deanna believed that she understood—when the volcano erupted, earthquakes would shake the ice fields and make the ground unstable. The wand would be helpful, but she wanted to be sure that she kept a tight grip on it.

While Deanna and Boldorf talked, Tobungus wrestled around in his non-shoe bag and dug out a puffy snow suit and a furry blanket to wrap around his mushroom cap head. He ended up looking like an inflated sleeping bag with a fuzzy top. Zorell had to bite his own tongue to stop himself from making fun of Tobungus' comical outfit.

The hike up the snow-packed ice fields was slow. The sun began to fall in the sky. Deanna knew that they would never reach the temple and finish their search before darkness came. She also sensed that she needed the snowhoppers' confidence. "I think we should stop here for the night," she said to Boldorf.

"My young friend," Boldorf said, "even snowhoppers would be uncomfortable this high up the mountain without shelter."

"I'll take care of the shelter," Deanna said softly. She reached into her pocket and pulled out a handful of small stones. She waved the wand over them and uttered a few words which the others could not hear. She threw the stones in a circle outside the group of snowhoppers and shouted, "*Constructo temperaro!*"

The snowhoppers looked on in awe as a curtain of orange light shot upward from the stones and then toward a spot over the center of the group. A tent of light kept the cold and snow out.

Derek smiled at Deanna and shook his head. "You're getting too good." Everyone clamored inside and rested peacefully for the night.

The next morning, the sun shone brightly, with only light snow falling from patchy clouds, and a strong wind blew from the far side of the mountain. As he brushed the last bits of sleep from his mind, Derek thought he caught the faintest strands of the drums that they had heard the day before. He looked over and saw Tobungus straining to hear.

"Yes, it's there," Tobungus whispered. "They know we're here." Tobungus' words sent a chill up Derek's back.

Moments later, the sounds of hundreds of snowhoppers stirring forced Derek to get up and see if Deanna was ready to resume their search for the temple. He found her near the center of the shelter talking with Boldorf about the rest of their journey. When everyone was ready, she flicked her wand and the shelter disappeared. The stones flew back into her hand and she returned them to her pocket.

Boldorf looked impressed, as he organized his snowhoppers into position to protect the party from any attack Eldrack might bring. Two of the snowhoppers rolled in the snow instead of joining the others. "Bimmi, Freedle," Boldorf squeaked, "over here, now!"

The two young snowhoppers stood before Boldorf who pulled out a small book. He flipped through the pages quickly. "Yes, here it is," he said. "The punishment for not protecting friends against a dark wizard." He reached into his pouch and pulled two snowballs out. He threw one at each of the small snowhoppers.

As the morning wore on, dozens of snowhoppers got in trouble with their leader. Each time, he looked in his book and then threw a snowball at the troublemaker.

Derek suspected that Boldorf simply liked throwing snowballs and didn't really care that the other snowhoppers were goofing around.

He also suspected that the snowhoppers liked getting hit by snowballs just as much as they liked throwing them. No one seemed to get hurt, and they all laughed as they toppled into the drifting snow.

The snow had been light when they started their hike to the temple, but it was getting heavier, and the winds were growing stronger. A full-blown blizzard was brewing.

Just after lunch, they reached a large mound of snow. Boldorf slapped his thick tail on the ground and proclaimed that they had reached the Temple of Ice.

"It's slightly less grand than I imagined," Derek blurted out.

"It snows here every day and every night," Boldorf replied quickly. "Snowhoppers, clear the Temple!"

The army of snowhoppers hopped to the snow mound and began slapping the ground with their tails. The combined force made the ground tremble. At first, small pockets of snow began to fall from the mound. Soon, large chunks peeled away. In only a few minutes, a beautiful building was exposed. Giant blocks of golden marble made up the walls. Colorful decorations hung below the huge wooden roof. Finally, the snowhoppers uncovered large purple doors guarded by pink marble columns.

Deanna walked slowly into the majestic temple of ice. Her jaw dropped at the details in the carvings and the colors of the jewels that dotted every surface. Volcanoes were a main theme in the carvings, and she had found a story about the volcano on the far side of Mount Drasius. As she viewed the story, she understood that the snowhoppers did not fear the volcano. They saw it as the twin brother of their beloved ice fields.

Meanwhile, Derek had found carvings about another volcano which he struggled to understand.

Two shapes caught his eye. They were wands; he was sure of it. He realized that this must be a story about the Kutama Volcano, a towering volcanic cone where lava mixes with water from a Ruby Well over a pit where the Wand of Ondarell and its sister wand were formed. He tried to figure out what the story meant, but it was confusing.

After the wands were formed, it looked like they were carried away by large birds. In the scenes that followed, there were battles between wizards who led armies of many types of creatures. The birds always flew above the battles, holding the wands. In the final scene, the battle was over and the wands were reunited, but he couldn't tell how it happened.

The snowhoppers slowly wandered into the temple and bowed their heads in a combination of awe and respect at the work of Tarook. In the cavernous temple that kept the sounds of the blizzard out of their minds, they lost all thoughts of snowball fights.

Boldorf proudly led the snowhoppers with his head held high. He approached Deanna and said, "I don't wish to rush you, but we are able to feel rumblings in the ground that you cannot sense. Our tails have special hairs that can feel tiny earthquakes. The ground is growing more restless, and I fear that soon, the far side will awaken."

"Of course," Deanna said. "I was amazed at the beauty of Tarook's Temple. I will speed up my search for the stone."

Deanna hurried over and told Derek that they needed to find the stone quickly, before the volcano erupted. Derek called Tobungus and Zorell over.

Derek was surprised to see Zorell and Tobungus standing near each other looking at other carvings. They appeared to have temporarily agreed to a truce and were actually working together. He told them to hurry up their search for any sign of the moonstone. They all went off in their own directions and looked at every shining jewel on the walls.

The minutes dragged on with no sign of the moonstone. Every few minutes, Deanna wondered if Eldrack had beaten them to it. She looked over and saw Derek staring at the ceiling. "What is it, Derek?" she asked.

"I was wondering if Tarook designed the openings in the ceiling for a reason," he answered. "Look. The light comes in and shines on the volcano carvings in each story. It looks like he wanted visitors to study each story panel. It's the only light in the room."

"No, it's not," Tobungus called out. Derek and Deanna looked over and saw the mushroom man pointing to a mound of snow in the center of the room. A faint white light glowed from inside it.

Zorell hopped on the pile of snow and dug it away like he was flicking away kitty litter. When he was done, they all saw a thick glass circle covering a pit that held the glowing, milky white moonstone that they had come to find.

# 8  Pillars, What Pillars?

"Well, there it is," Tobungus said. "But how do we get it?"

"There's always magic," Deanna said. She pulled the wand out and pointed it at the clear covering. Her first spell was a fiery blast that she thought would burn through the glass. The beam reflected off of the surface and bounced around the room, scattering snowhoppers as it zapped the floor.

Next, she tried to melt the cover, but the spell bounced off and melted Derek's hat instead. Finally, she tried to simply move the cover away with a spell. Again, the spell deflected off and hit Tobungus who went bouncing around the Temple.

Before Deanna could think of another spell, the floor shook. "The beast is awake," Boldorf proclaimed.

Derek looked through the doorway and saw an orange glow from the other side of the mountain. "Deanna, we better hurry up," he said.

"Okay, magic isn't working," she muttered to herself. "Think!"

"Does anybody notice something missing?" Zorell asked.

"What do you mean?" Derek replied hopefully.

"The story you read mentioned the seven pillars of Tarook's Temple. I don't see any pillars."

Everyone looked around and saw that he was right. Another earthquake shook the Temple. This one was stronger than the last.

"Boldorf," Deanna shouted across the room, "Come over here, please."

The head snowhopper hopped to Deanna's side with three mighty strides. "How may I help you?" he asked seriously.

"We noticed that there aren't any pillars here, but the book we read said that there were seven pillars. Do you know where the pillars are?"

"No, I'm afraid I don't," Boldorf answered.

"Well, then, do you know if Tarook finished this Temple before he disappeared?" Deanna asked.

"Absolutely, this is his crowning achievement," Boldorf said.

"Yes, it is grand," Deanna said respectfully. "But, how can you be so sure that he finished every last detail?"

"On very special days, we tell stories about Tarook," Boldorf said. "As a leader, it is my job to make sure that the other snowhoppers know about Tarook. When Tarook was building this Temple, he would come to the snowhopper villages to rest and get supplies. He would always stop to tell my grandfather about the progress he had made and his plans for the next areas of the temple. I was a small boy, but I remember every one of his stories."

"On one glorious day, he came and announced that he was done. His words filled our people with pride. He told us that his Temple would rise from the ice fields. Then, he disappeared."

"Thank you," Deanna said. "It looks like we have a mystery on our hands."

"Deanna," Derek called, "Look at the ceiling." The quakes were getting more frequent and stronger. "There are seven circles spread out around the outside edges of the ceiling. It looks like places for the pillars."

"Could the pillars be invisible?" Tobungus wondered. He ran to one of the places where a pillar would be and launched himself into the air. He flew right through and rolled on the floor. "I guess there's no invisible pillar here," he said sheepishly.

"What are we missing?" Deanna said, rubbing her head.

"Wait a minute," Derek said. "The key's in Boldorf's story." Everyone looked at him hopefully. "Boldorf, you said that Tarook told your people that he finished the Temple, right?"

"Yes, that's right," Boldorf answered proudly.

"Okay, but he also told you that the Temple would rise from the ice fields," Derek added.

"Yes, and here it is, as you can see," Boldorf said.

"No, the Temple is on the ice fields. It is part of it. It has not yet risen." Turning to Deanna, he said, "I bet the pillars will rise from the floor and rest in those circles. When they do, they will make the Temple rise from the ice fields. The moonstone will be freed from its case underneath the Temple."

"Boldorf," Derek said, "The whole purpose of the Temple is to protect the moonstone."

"That can't be," Boldorf said. He thought that Derek did not understand the importance of the drawings on the walls. They showed the snowhoppers their history. He tried to tell Derek this as quickly as he could.

"No, Boldorf," Derek said, "The Temple is not for the snowhoppers at all."

Boldorf straightened up and was about to argue with Derek.

"Please, Boldorf, don't misunderstand what I am saying" Derek said. "You and the other snowhopper leaders show your people the history. You tell them the stories that are shown on the walls of the temple. Your people don't come to the temple to learn about snowhopper history. They don't need to. Tarook put the stories here for the wizards who would be sent for the moonstone so that we would understand. The stories are for us."

Boldorf thought through what Derek was saying. He realized that what Derek said meant that Tarook was important far beyond the lands of the snowhoppers. Tarook had been entrusted with one of the vital moonstones that would play a part in the ultimate battle for Elestra.

"You honor us with your understanding," Boldorf said to Derek.

Deanna opened her locket and the Book of Spells appeared in front of her. She wasn't sure what type of spell to use. She skimmed the pages, but was coming up empty.

Zorell peeked out the door. To one side, he saw the volcanic glow getting brighter. On the snowy side, he saw movement that did not look like snowhoppers. "Deanna," he said, "I must encourage you to hurry up. I think that we will have an unwelcome visitor very soon."

"How do I get pillars to grow?" Deanna whispered to herself. She searched the paintings on the walls and saw that most of them contained images of trees.

"That's it," she shouted. "I have to make the pillars grow like trees." She aimed the wand at the ground under the nearest circle and uttered the words *arboreus acceleratum*. A tree-like pillar made of green marble began to rise from the floor. She quickly repeated the spell at the six other locations.

As Deanna worked, Derek continued looking at the images on the walls. He sensed that the stories were important to understanding their role in Elestra's future. But, he knew that he would never be able to remember them all.

"Tobungus," he yelled. "Use your picture ball to get pictures of everything on these walls."

Tobungus was happy to be useful again and threw the ball in a wild arc around the room.

The pillars had just reached the ceiling when the floor began to rumble, even more than it had from the earthquakes. To everyone in the room, it looked like pure magical power was flowing from Deanna, making the pillars grow more and more quickly. The pillars lifted the Temple nearly thirty feet into the air.

Tobungus looked out the door and saw the

huge drop to the ground and said, "Okay, the moonstone is free. Now how do we get down to get it?"

# 9  One Happy Cat

"Oh, man," Derek muttered. "We're pretty high up. I don't think we can jump."

"Zorell might land on his feet and Tobungus looks like he's sealed in bubble wrap," Deanna said, "but we'd never make it."

"You must know some kind of spell to make a staircase or a flying carpet or something," Derek said anxiously.

Deanna looked down in time to see a wave of snow fall from the temple's roof and smash into hundreds of snowhoppers below. They were carried more than a mile down the mountain, toward their village.

"It's time for me to get down there," Boldorf said. "Each of you, get on a snowhopper's back and we'll jump down. Guardian Deanna, I would be honored if you would ride on my back."

Deanna climbed onto Boldorf's back, and the others mounted their snowhoppers. They didn't know what to expect, but the powerful creatures were amazing jumpers. They felt like they were floating, as the snowhoppers used their tails to guide their descent. Their landings were soft, and

Derek and Deanna hopped off of their rides immediately.

They ran under the Temple with Tobungus and Zorell following. Deanna had the wand out, waiting to get close enough to aim a spell accurately. Derek scanned the underside of the Temple to plan their best line of defense, if it really was Eldrack that Zorell had seen down the mountain.

The ground was rumbling more strongly than ever with almost constant tremors. They could now hear the roar of the volcanic eruption over the whipping blizzard winds. Deanna dropped to her knees in front of the thick casing around the moonstone. A small seam caught her eye. She quickly understood what Tarook had done. He created a series of layers around the moonstone.

There must have been at least ten separate layers that she would have to remove. She wasn't sure if she would be able to use the same spell each time, or if she would need to find a new spell to work on each layer. With no time to waste, she began peeling the moonstone's protection away.

Deanna's hands were turning red from the bitterly cold wind and snow, and the wand shook as she pointed it at the casing around the moonstone. She took a break to blow on her hands to warm them a bit, but quickly went back to work.

A clump of snow landed on Derek's shoulder, and his first thought was that the snowhoppers had picked a really bad time for a snowball fight. Instead, he looked up and saw sections of snow falling from the Temple, which was shaking on its pillars. The tremors from the volcano were growing stronger, and he wasn't sure how long the Temple could stay up without collapsing on them. "Deanna, you'd better hurry," he called.

"I'm going as fast as I can," she called back.

"Go faster," Tobungus screamed across the area under the Temple. Deanna looked up angrily. She was ready to yell at the mushroom man, but she saw that he was pointing at a dark figure emerging from the snow storm. Eldrack had arrived.

Deanna pulled the wand away from her work on the moonstone and prepared to fire a spell at the dark wizard. Before she could shout the words of the spell she had chosen, she looked down and saw that the last layer she had removed had started to reappear.

"Derek," she cried, "I can't stop working on this, or the case will reappear."

"Call Gretz out," Derek called. "Maybe he can weaken the connections between the layers of the case."

"Good idea," Deanna said. She reached into her backpack and grabbed the rusty chain that held Gretz's tiny workshop. She knocked on the glowing workshop ball, and the little Fixer popped out.

"How can I help?" Gretz asked before realizing that they were in great danger under the temple. He looked around and saw Eldrack in the distance.

"Can you help me remove this casing from the moonstone?" Deanna yelled over the whipping wind.

Gretz looked at Eldrack again, picked up his tool box, and said, "So sorry, but I have far too much puttering to do." He zipped back into his tiny workshop and hummed so loudly that Deanna could hear him over the sound of the raging storm.

"Gretz is no help here," Deanna called.

"Okay," Derek replied, "I'll try to think of something. Before he could do anything, he saw Eldrack raise his wand toward the Temple. He was still far enough away, that Derek thought his aim would be off. A beam of purple light shot from his wand and flew past Deanna's right ear. It hit one of the pillars. The Temple continued to shake, and they could hear the pillars creaking.

Eldrack's next shot was aimed toward

Tobungus. This one missed, instead hitting another of the pillars.

Deanna looked up for a couple of seconds to see what was happening. Before she could think through the situation, she dove back into her work. She was already through five layers. *I'm halfway there,* she thought.

Derek's mind wandered to the socks that they had bought in Amemnop. What if he used those against Eldrack? But then, what if Eldrack knew the type of magic they held? Derek grabbed his backpack. He realized that it was his only chance.

He pulled one of the socks out and waited for Eldrack to choose his next target. The dark wizard seemed to be pointing his wand at Deanna. As soon as Eldrack's wand jumped to life, Derek threw the balled-up sock and hit the beam of magical light. The sock exploded in a bright white light, and became a column of ice in front of Deanna.

Deanna looked up and saw what Derek had done. She nodded to him to let him know how impressed she was. The column was helping to hold up the Temple, and it gave Deanna protection from Eldrack's blasts.

"That was a fine bit of magic," Boldorf said from behind Derek.

"Yeah, it worked for now," Derek said. "But what I'm worried about is when Deanna tries to get out from under the Temple." Derek had already moved halfway toward the edge of the area covered by the Temple.

"Wizard," Boldorf said, "I have a plan."

Derek felt a surge of pride at being called wizard. He listened to Boldorf's plan and gave the snowhopper another magical sock. Boldorf called the remaining snowhoppers over and quickly told them his plan.

The Temple was rocking back and forth on its pillars. The ice column that Derek had created was starting to crack. There wasn't much time left. Under the center of the Temple, Deanna was still focusing on the moonstone. The case around it was much thinner than when she started. It looked like she was on the final layer.

Outside, Eldrack was still firing bolts from his wand, but he seemed to have terrible aim in the snow storm. The ground shook more violently than earlier, and the Temple started to make a low rumbling sound, like it was falling in on its legs.

"Deanna!" Derek called. "You've got to get out of there. The Temple's about to collapse."

"I've got it," Deanna yelled, holding the moonstone up high. "Everyone get out from under the Temple." Zorell and Tobungus had stayed underneath to act as decoys for Eldrack's blasts. All three of them ran toward safety outside the Temple area.

As soon as they started moving, Boldorf's snowhoppers charged at Eldrack to distract him. It worked perfectly. He stopped firing at Deanna, so she had a clear path to freedom. Eldrack fired wildly, trying to scatter the snowhoppers. He didn't feel the one that got behind him and slid the sock under his cape.

"Deanna," Derek called, "Throw me the wand." She looked confused. "Just do it! I know what I'm doing." Under his breath, he added, "I hope I know what I'm doing." She tossed the wand which landed in his outstretched hand. He turned toward Eldrack and raised the wand. *"Cryolius magnus!"* he bellowed. A swirling cloud of white light surrounded Eldrack. When the light faded, Eldrack was encased in ice.

Deanna reached the edge of the covered area at the same moment as Zorell. They looked back and saw Tobungus struggling with his puffy coat that looked like a giant marshmallow surrounding him. A huge chunk of stone fell near the center of the Temple. The building was crumbling. One of the pillars disintegrated under the weight of the

Temple. Tobungus would never make it out.

Zorell smiled. His chance had come. He ran back into the covered area, dodging falling debris on his way to Tobungus. As he reached his target, Tobungus was ready to collapse from exhaustion. Zorell took a cord from Tobungus' coat in his mouth and pulled the mushroom man to safety. As they emerged from the covered area, the Temple completely collapsed back to the ground.

Derek looked down at Tobungus who was lying on the ground sobbing, "No!" He looked over at Zorell who had the most satisfied look he had ever seen.

"And now, Mayor of Moldville, we are even," Zorell purred.

Tobungus' reign over Zorell had ended too quickly.

"We have to get out of here," Derek said to Deanna, leaving the old foes to resume their bickering.

"Give me the wand," Deanna said. She took it and pointed it at Eldrack who still stood frozen. Derek couldn't hear her words, but a massive blast shot from the wand and carried Eldrack so far down the mountain that they lost sight of him. "Now we should thank Boldorf for his help and get going," she said.

"Excuse me, Wizards," Zorell said, "If you want to thank Boldorf and honor him for his help, you must throw a snowball at him."

Derek's face broke into a huge grin. "With pleasure," he said. He picked up a snowball and threw it at the snowhopper leader. Boldorf bowed his head, and said, "It has been our great honor to serve with you against the dark wizard."

Derek and Deanna led their party down the mountain and back to Amemnop where they would take the fourth moonstone and place it in the arch at the top of the Tower of the Moons.

# 10 A New Shadow

The trip back to Amemnop included two very different conversations. Tobungus and Zorell had fallen back into their constant insults. Neither would admit it, but they were happiest when they were bickering with each other.

Derek and Deanna said very little. It was really Deanna who chose to be quiet. Derek watched his sister, but wasn't sure why she seemed to be somewhere between mad, sad, and scared. Every time he tried to ask her what was wrong, she said, "I don't want to talk about it right now."

Derek let his mind wander to his first real use of magic. He was proud of his quick thinking, but he knew that next time, Eldrack would be ready for him. Still, he thought that Eldrack's attack should put Deanna's mind at ease about the dark wizard's plans.

When they reached Amemnop, Deanna led them straight to Glabber's. She told Tobungus and Zorell to get some dinner and led Derek outside. She wanted to get the moonstone to the Tower before they ate. She also was almost ready to talk to Derek about what was bothering her.

The walk to the Tower of the Moons seemed like a normal evening walk back in their home town. They both felt a little bit of sadness at the thought of their parents. They knew that their parents could not come to Elestra because Eldrack would sense their presence and capture them. As they got closer, Deanna picked up her pace, and was almost running up the stairs when they entered the Tower.

She carefully took the moonstone out, and looked through it at the fourth moon. She handed it to Derek, and he felt the warm rush of magical energy wash over him as he looked at the fourth moon's light. She took the moonstone back and slipped it into the arch where it joined its three sister stones that had been placed there after earlier adventures. Deanna looked at the line of moonstones and felt like they were finally making a dent in their journey.

Derek cleared his throat. "Are you alright, Deanna?" he asked softly.

"Yeah, I guess so," she answered. "It's just that I can't get the thought of being under the Temple out of my mind. It was pretty scary. It was like I had no control."

Derek thought about what it must have been like in the center of the Temple with Eldrack firing bolts of magical fire at Deanna. "Well, you made it and saved the moonstone," Derek said.

"Yeah," Deanna replied. "No one said these adventures would be easy."

"And, we know something else," Derek added. Deanna looked at him to see what he meant. "We know that we don't have to question Eldrack's motives anymore."

"What do you mean?" Deanna asked.

"Deanna, he tried to fry you," Derek blurted out. "It doesn't get any clearer than that. He aimed his wand right at you and fired several times. He aimed at all of us. You're just lucky that Tarook's pillars stood up against his blasts."

"No, Derek," Deanna sighed. "That's another thing that's bothering me. Eldrack didn't attack us. He used his magic to keep the pillars standing."

"That's impossible," Derek muttered.

"Derek, Eldrack is supposed to be THE dark wizard. He's imprisoned thirteen generations of our family. That's a lot of power. Do you really think that he would miss so many times?" Before Derek could answer, she continued, "And didn't you notice that all of his spells hit the pillars? None of them fell until I got out."

"So does that mean that Eldrack's on our

side?" Derek whispered.

"No," Deanna said strongly, "it means that he didn't want me to be crushed under the Temple. We don't know why, but we have to find out."

"Wait a minute, Deanna," Derek said, "if you thought that, why did you hit him with such a powerful blast after he was frozen?"

"I didn't use a spell that would hurt him," Deanna answered. "I knocked him down the mountain—away from the eruption. I made sure that the spell would make his icy covering melt, but only after we were far enough away."

"You know, Deanna," Derek said. "There's another possibility here."

"What do you mean?" Deanna asked, hoping that Derek had some idea that would make Eldrack's actions make sense.

"Think about the prophecy, Deanna" Derek said, just above a whisper. "Eldrack may know that he is not strong enough to defeat the king alone. He may need you, or us, to join him. Maybe he is trying to convince you that he's not so bad, so that you'll join him."

"Don't you mean so that we'll join him?" Deanna shot back.

"Of course, Deanna," Derek said. "I just hate the thought of joining him."

"So do I, Derek," Deanna said. "I know that he's our enemy, but it's hard to figure out everything he does. I mean, he's frozen our family in that moving cave. He made Amemnop feel like a darkened prison. Just because I didn't get crushed under the temple doesn't mean I'd think that suddenly he's changed his ways. For all we know, he may have been worried that the moonstone would be lost under the temple."

"Or, maybe he knows something about the spells that Tarook put on the temple," Derek said. "It's possible that Eldrack thought that only you could get the stone out. He's very powerful, Deanna. There may be prophecies about the moonstones that only he has seen."

"Maybe you can ask Gula Badu the next time you wander down into the archives," Deanna said.

"Look, this is all pretty confusing," Derek muttered. "Why don't we go to Glabber's and get something to eat. I'm starving, and maybe we can talk to Iszarre about Eldrack."

"That sounds like a good idea," Deanna agreed. "I'm starved too. Maybe we'll get lucky and Glabber will make us pizza again."

They made their way out of the Tower and back to Glabber's. When they entered the Grub Hut, all thoughts of food left their minds. They were shocked to see that a crowd had gathered around something that looked like a boxing ring near the far wall. When they made their way ringside, they saw Tobungus and Zorell with boxing gloves trying to have a boxing match.

Tobungus' arms were so short that he couldn't punch Zorell. He looked more like he was shivering. Zorell's paws were so small that his punches tickled Tobungus. Even though they couldn't hit each other, the two fighters talked trash the whole time. Derek laughed in disbelief when he saw that there were actually people cheering for Zorell or Tobungus.

After seven rounds, both fighters fell to the ground in exhaustion. They had not actually hit each other, but talking nonstop had worn them out. Derek and Deanna pulled them out of the ring.

"Come with me," Deanna said. She led the two out through the front door.

"Where are we going?" Tobungus panted.

"You two need to cool off," Deanna replied. Before they could say anything, Deanna raised the wand toward them and shouted, *"Launcheum Fountainus!"*

Tobungus and Zorell flew high into the air all the way to the Fountain of the Six Kingdoms. They splashed into the cold water, shouting, sputtering, and shivering as they fought to get to the edge. They forgot their battle and thought only about getting dry.

"Come on," Deanna said to Derek, "Now we'll have peace and quiet when we talk to Iszarre. They went back in and ordered one of Glabber's huge meals and made sure to ask for pizza. They asked the snake chef to have Iszarre come to see them when he was free.

"I'm afraid that Iszarre is not here right now," Glabber hissed.

"Do you know when he'll be back?" Deanna asked.

"Oh," Glabber said, looking out a window at the front of the diner, "He should return in about two hours."

After Glabber had slithered back into the kitchen, Derek said suddenly, "Deanna, we forgot to watch the vision through the moonstone."

"Oh, man," Deanna said, "How could we have forgotten? Let's go back to the tower now so we can be back when Iszarre returns."

"But, what about the pizza?" Derek asked.

"We can eat with Iszarre when he returns," Deanna replied.

Derek nodded, and they headed back out into the Amemnop evening.

# The Fourth Vision

Derek and Deanna left the Grub Hut and walked in the warm Elestran night toward the Tower of the Moons. They were feeling safer and more familiar with the great city.

The climb to the top of the tower took longer than usual because they were so tired from their adventure. They were also a bit nervous about what they would see in their vision.

As they approached the fourth moonstone, they both took a deep breath and brought their heads together to peer into the magical stone.

A blinding flash of light started their vision. They were in Tarook's temple. This time, it felt like they were really there. They could hear and feel everything.

There had been something silly about the snowhoppers they had seen when they went to the mountain. Boldorf and his people were all throwing snowballs and yipping excitedly. In the vision, they saw a snowhopper who was different. This one looked wise, and he was not fooling around with snowballs.

"That must be Tarook," Derek whispered, but he wasn't sure if he really said the words or if he thought them as they watched the vision.

Tarook's wand looked like an icicle. As he pointed it toward the moonstone, beams of white energy swirled around. The layers of the case were being created.

"You must work faster," an old man urged. Derek and Deanna realized that this man was Pontifree, the fourth Mystical Guardian. He was short, and even when he seemed rushed and nervous, he had a happy look on his face.

"I'm going as fast as I can," Tarook said. "If I get this wrong, the moonstone will not be protected."

A noise, somewhere across the room, caught everyone's attention. It sounded like a tool fell. It was not much more than a clanking sound, but it seemed out of place to everyone who heard it.

Derek and Deanna saw Tarook and Pontifree staring at a statue near the far wall. They thought they saw movement by the statue, but they couldn't be sure.

The next thing they heard was Pontifree rushing past them. He called back to Tarook, "I'll hold him off! Finish the case!"

Tarook looked up for a couple of very long seconds and then turned back to the case he was creating.

Before Pontifree could get halfway across the room, Eldrack stepped out from behind the statue. "Pontifree, we can make this easy or we can make this difficult," the dark wizard bellowed. "It's your choice."

"Nothing's ever easy with you," Pontifree replied. He raised his wand and shot waves of freezing spells at Eldrack.

Eldrack raised his wand at the same time and created something that looked like a huge mirror in front of him. The freezing spells bounced back and encased Pontifree in ice. "Oh, come on. That was too easy," Eldrack muttered.

Eldrack turned his attention to Tarook who had just finished the final layer of the case surrounding the moonstone. "I suppose that you've created some sort of magical covering to protect the moonstone from evil," he called out.

"That's right, Eldrack," Tarook said in a low voice. "The moonstone is safe until it is time for the union of the stones."

"We shall see about that," Eldrack hissed. "And now, what to do with you?"

Tarook hopped away toward an opening to the snowy mountain outside the temple. When he reached the exit, he looked back to see if Eldrack was following him. To his surprise, Eldrack was still standing in the center of the temple watching the snowhopper wizard escape.

Tarook took a few steps out into the snow and was quickly snatched up by a dragon that swooped out of the blizzard. Back in the temple, Eldrack smiled. He knew that he had captured not only another Mystical Guardian, but also a very powerful snowhopper wizard who was being carried away into the unending whiteness of the storm.

The vision faded. Derek and Deanna looked at each other. They understood why Tarook had not been seen by the snowhoppers.

"I wonder if Eldrack has Tarook in the Cave of Imprisonment," Derek said.

"Probably," Deanna said. "That dragon is something that worries me. It's one thing to have knifebirds and gong beaters, but a huge dragon dropping from the sky? That's a pretty scary thought."

"Yeah, I don't think I'd like to run into one of those." Derek shuddered. "Listen, let's get back and see if Iszarre has returned.

They walked back to Glabber's quickly. They were trying to think about the vision, but their minds were still on Eldrack's actions when they were at the temple.

The Grub Hut was almost empty when they walked in. They chose a table as far from the other customers as possible. Glabber saw them and brought drinks and five different pizzas to their table. Glabber must have sensed that the twins were still troubled by something because the toppings were all recognizable—cheese, mushrooms, pineapple chunks, and olives.

"Thanks, Glabber," Deanna said.

"You're quite welcome," Glabber hissed. "When you have finished your dinner, I have a dessert pizza for you," he added, pointing the end of his tail at the counter, where there was a pizza covered with chunks of butter, puddles of honey, friddleberries, peekaboo peppers, and tiny red seeds that sang a happy tune as they danced around the crust.

"Has Iszarre returned?" Derek asked, before taking a bite of mushroom and olive pizza.

"Yes," Glabber replied. "I'll let him know that you wish to see him." He slithered into the kitchen.

Iszarre appeared a few minutes later and sensed that Deanna's mind was clouded. "I hope you are not depressed because Gonoolian Flort Beetles are out of season," he said sincerely. She looked confused by his comment. "Okay, then, why are you troubled?"

"There's something that I can't figure out about Eldrack," Deanna said.

"My dear Deanna," Iszarre said, "Eldrack does not have Flort Beetles."

"No, it's not about Eldrack having Flort Beetles," she began.

Iszarre interrupted her, "Although, I'm sure that Eldrack has had Flort Beetles. Well, who hasn't." He sat back with his hands locked across his stomach. "I remember the Flort Beetle Festivals back in the days before the plagues of Wisnian Trapper Flowers."

"What?" Derek blurted out.

"Oh, that's right, you're probably used to plagues of bugs eating plants," Iszarre explained. "Like locusts eating crops. Here in Elestra, we have plants that trap and eat bugs. Every once in a while, we have a plague of those plants and they eat huge numbers of bugs. After the last plague, we have been left with a shortage of Flort Beetles. That's why we can only eat them in season. It's not because of Eldrack."

"Hold on," Deanna said. "I am not concerned with Flort Beetles. I am trying to figure out why it seems that Eldrack tried to save me from being crushed by Tarook's Temple. This isn't the first time that it seems like Eldrack has avoided hurting us."

"My dear," Iszarre said in a voice barely above a whisper, "You must not question that Eldrack is your enemy." Deanna was about to argue, but Iszarre held up his hand. "No, you must listen to me. Eldrack is very clever. He may be trying to make you think that he is not an evil dark wizard. He might want to convince you to work with him. He has seen your power. Everyone has. I'll say it again—don't question that Eldrack is your enemy."

"But, Iszarre," Derek said, "Deanna has a point. He could have crushed her under the Temple and taken the moonstone."

Iszarre leaned closer to them, and whispered, "You may bring your concerns to me, but never speak of this to anyone else. I have no doubt that after you find the final moonstone you will see Eldrack for what he is. You will then stand with the forces of good against the evil that threatens the future of Elestra."

Before Deanna could say anything, an orange bird landed on their table. "Ah," Iszarre said, "to what do we owe the honor of your visit?"

The bird flew up into the air and exploded in

a bright flash. In its place, an eight foot tall man with green spiky hair stood before them. "I come from the Court of King Barado." He bowed slowly. "The King has taken special notice of your contributions to the safety of the Kingdom. You are hereby invited to visit the King in two days for a picnic."

Deanna and Derek looked confused. Iszarre explained, "This is a great honor. In Elestra, picnics are like feasts in your world."

The messenger continued, "When you are at the palace, the King will allow you to use the Screaming Elestran Newts to send a message to your parents."

Without warning, the man turned back into a bird and flew away. In response to their stunned silence, Iszarre told them that the newts could send a message between worlds by letting out incredibly loud screams that could cut through the magical atmospheres that protected each world.

"Deanna," Iszarre said, continuing their conversation as if an eight-foot tall exploding bird had not interrupted them. "You are concerned that Eldrack might not really be the evil wizard that you thought he was." Deanna nodded. "Is that what the vision told you?"

"What do you mean?" Deanna asked.

"I get it," Derek said. Deanna looked at him. "Eldrack knew that Tarook protected the moonstone from him. There was no way he could get it. He had to wait for you to get it."

Deanna nodded slowly as if she was following his train of thought and took another bite of pizza. "He was probably going to attack you after you had the moonstone freed from its casing."

"I guess you're right," Deanna said, even though she still thought that there was something not quite right about this explanation.

Her thoughts were interrupted by Derek asking, "Iszarre, what did Tarook mean by the union of the stones?"

"There is a prophecy, Derek, that says that the moonstones will be brought together when the great battle approaches," Iszarre replied. He saw that Derek was about to ask another question, so he added, "Now, don't go asking anything else. You will find the prophecy when the time is right."

"But, didn't you just tell us the prophecy?" Deanna asked.

"Yes and no," Iszarre answered.

"This is about to get frustrating," Derek said. "Deanna, he can't tell us any more because we are in the prophecy. Just drop it for now, and maybe Gula Badu will show me the prophecy when we're at the library."

"Fine," Deanna said. "We've got a lot to think about without another prophecy to confuse us."

"Well, you two should get some sleep," Iszarre said. "I'm sure that you have another long day at the library ahead of you tomorrow."

Derek and Deanna were so tired that they didn't argue. They dragged themselves up to their room and fell into their beds. They both fell asleep instantly. Derek had a dream of a long dark tunnel. He recognized it as the entrance to the room where Gula Badu had shown him the prophecies.

Deanna had a dream about the same tunnel, but in her dream, she saw Derek walk toward the door to the Archive of the Prophecies. He turned and told her to wait a minute.

Derek dreamt that Gula Badu told him about their next quest. In Deanna's dream, she saw Derek come out of the Archive. He walked over and told her what he had heard.

They both woke up instantly and said, "The Eye of the Red Dragon."

Turn the page.  The adventure continues…

# Epilogue

Derek and Deanna have now found the first four moonstones and defeated Eldrack and his minions in Amemnop, the Atteelian Orchard, the Desert Realm, and on Mt. Drasius, but there is much more to do and much more to learn.

In their bits of free time, Deanna and Derek continue to wander through the State Library of Magia to find out more about the places, people, and creatures they have encountered. The following pages will tell you what they learned, or perhaps what they didn't learn.

# Magical Connections

Derek and Deanna spent the rest of the night trying to get back to sleep, but the thought of meeting up with a group of dragons kept them awake. When the last of the moons had set and the sun was just peeking above the horizon, Derek gave up and opened the curtains. A few people were already on the streets, and the sounds of Glabber and Iszarre getting ready for the breakfast crowd crept up through the floorboards.

Deanna yawned and said, "I never thought I'd say this, but I'm hungry for some of Glabber's cooking."

"As long as he doesn't hide another peekaboo pepper in my food," Derek said. "I don't need another surprise this morning."

"What do you mean, another surprise?" Deanna asked.

"The dream telling us that we have to go to the Dragon Realm was a surprise, don't you think?" Derek replied.

"Oh, yeah, I guess we have had a surprise already today," Deanna said. "The idea of facing dragons is a little scary. I think we should get going so we can learn as much as possible to be ready for tomorrow."

They got ready and gathered their things for a day in Amemnop. Deanna put her headband on, and it seemed like the moons vibrated slightly when they touched her hair. She suddenly felt like the headband was more than something to keep her hair in place. She touched it gently. "Derek," she said, "make sure you bring your bracelet."

"Huh?" Derek said, as he shoved his special candles into his backpack.

"The bracelet that grandpa gave you," Deanna answered. "I think my headband has some kind of power, and I bet that your bracelet does too. I think we should be sure to take them with us wherever we go in Elestra."

"Sure," Derek said. He put his bracelet on, but he didn't notice anything about it that made him think that it held any special power.

They went down to the dining room and ate a remarkably normal meal of fruit and pancakes. Before Tobungus or Zorell could show up, the twins left the Grub Hut and made their way to the library.

When they reached the fairy librarian's desk, Derek didn't wait to find out if Deanna had any ideas about what they should study. "Can we see books about magical connections and types of magic?" he asked.

"Well, those are two separate issues," the fairy librarian replied. "But, I'm sure that we can find a few books that can give you the basic information that you'll need."

The swarm of book fairies exploded out from under the desk and zipped up to find books whose titles were glowing. One by one, books floated down to the table where Derek and Deanna were sitting.

When the last book settled on top of the stack, Derek said, "We'd like to learn about magical connections, or maybe how fixers work on magical connections."

A large brown book with a picture of a tiny workshop like Gretz's slid off of the pile and rested in front of Deanna. *"Explanatum!"* she said.

They were used to the books opening up and telling them what they needed to know, but this book was different. The picture of the workshop began to glow and a man who was about Gretz's height popped out next to their table.

"Good evening, or morning, or maybe afternoon," the little man said. "I can't really tell what time of day it is in this library."

"It's morning," Deanna said. "Does this book talk like the rest of the books here?"

"Even better," the fixer said. "Sit back and

enjoy the show." He touched various spots on the book's cover and mumbled a series of strange words that Deanna didn't recognize. When he was done, he started to walk toward the back of the library.

"Where are you going?" Derek asked.

"I've been in that workshop a long time," the fixer said. "I have to run to the bathroom while you're watching the book." He turned and kept walking.

"Watching the book?" Deanna whispered to Derek.

Before Derek could reply, the book whipped its cover open and a rainbow of light started to swirl above its pages. The hazy light came together and the image of a wizard stood on the open book. A voice said, "The most basic way to use magic is to say the words of a spell and to wave a wand."

The tiny holographic wizard said, "*Pyrofloris.*" A jet of sparks shot upward like miniature fireworks and exploded in the shapes of beautiful flowers over the table.

The tiny wizard faded away and then reappeared in front of the image of a castle's gate. "Sometimes, a wizard needs to use magic on an object," the book said. "This castle gate that you see is filled with magic that keeps intruders out. The wizard uses spells that mix with the gate's magic to open the gate."

The tiny wizard waved his wand, but the gate remained closed. He tried again, but nothing happened.

"The magic is in the gate, but it is a mix of different types of magic, and they can't connect because something is broken," the book explained. "A fixer can study the magical connections and fix any that are broken."

A holographic fixer suddenly appeared next to the wizard and opened his tool box. He fiddled around with the gate and the arch surrounding it. When he was done, the wizard waved his wand again. This time, the gate opened. The tiny wizard and fixer looked at Derek and Deanna and smiled.

While the book began to explain what the fixer had done, the little fixer hopped off of the book and started to walk across the table. "Hey, get back here," the book called.

The wizard pointed his wand at the fixer and shouted, "*Returnio!*" The little fixer hovered above the table and floated back to the holographic scene over the book.

"Sometimes, there are pockets of one type of magic that doesn't mix well with other types," the book said. "For instance, lightning magic and rock magic don't mix at all."

The little holographic wizard was walking along a path. Up ahead, he saw a snarling 37-toothed water weasel hiding behind a pile of rocks. He raised his wand and fired a bolt of lightning toward the weasel. The lightning reached the rocks and disappeared.

The tiny fixer ran ahead and looked at the rocks. He walked back to the wizard and stood in front of him shaking his head disapprovingly. Finally, he turned and walked back to the rocks. He pulled out a spray bottle and sprayed a blue liquid on the rocks which disintegrated into sand.

The wizard shot another bolt of lightning. This time, it hit the weasel which started to growl and charge at the wizard.

"The fixer removed the rock magic, and the rocks fell apart," the book said. "That allowed the wizard to use his lightning spell. But, as you can see, a fixer can't make a wizard make the right decisions about whether to attack a 37-toothed water weasel or leave it alone."

The weasel was chasing the wizard all over the open pages of the book, occasionally nipping at his long robe. "I think I'd better close my pages and settle these two down," the book said. The hologram disappeared suddenly when the cover closed.

"Wow," Deanna said, sitting back in her chair for a moment. The library had gone startlingly quiet when the book's cover had closed. "Well, let's move on to types of magic. Do any of you books know about the types of magic?"

A maroon booked hopped down and said, "You want to know about the types of magic? That's pretty simple stuff, isn't it?" It sounded quite disappointed.

"We're new here," Deanna said. "And, yes, we would like to know about the types of magic."

The book snorted and said, "What type of voice should I use? I can do snooty, smarmy, insulting, bored, or distracted."

"Just tell us what we need to know," Derek blurted out.

"No can do, Skippy," the book said. Derek straightened up, ready to yell at the book. "Don't get excited. I'll tell you what you need to know, and then maybe someday, you'll learn how to do a few neat little magic tricks." The book opened up to its third page and said,

> "There are many types of magic in Elestra, and no one is sure that every type has been found. The main types are water, fire, tree, lightning,

*wind, ice, soil, and heat.*

*There are many more types of magic that are not used as often, such as rock, worm, sponge, moss, lint, bubble, paper, citrus, fur, and so on. Most things in Elestra have a little bit of unique magic. Many wizards spend years trying to figure out how tiny bits of magic from everyday items can make their spells stronger.*

*The strongest wizards study the types of magic to learn which types mix the best and which types don't mix at all. If they try to combine two types that don't mix, their spells will be weak."*

The book stopped reading its own words, and said, "Is that enough? I really do have a busy schedule."

"Sure, that told us enough for now," Deanna said.

"Good!" the book said. "Well, I hope someone can figure out how to use a spell to get me back to my shelf."

Deanna raised the wand and slowly said, "*Returnius shelfarro.*" The book flew like a missile to its spot on the shelves and came to a sudden stop.

"That'll work," the book said with a nervous voice that was much different than the snooty tone it used when it spoke to them.

"I've had enough of this subject," Deanna said, laughing at the book that seemed to have learned its lesson.

"I agree," Derek added. "Let's go talk to the librarian about a new stack of books."

# The Power of the Mystical Guardians

"What should we look up next?" Deanna said. She hadn't thought about what they should read about after their adventure with the snowhoppers.

"I know what I want to find out," Derek said. Deanna looked at him with a curious expression. "Have you noticed how the Mystical Guardians seemed weak against Eldrack in all of the visions?" He saw that Deanna was thinking back to what they had seen.

"I guess so," she said.

"They always seem to be running away with Eldrack having no problem defeating them," Derek said. "I want to find out if they really were weak or if Eldrack figured out some way to defeat them easily."

"That makes a lot of sense," Deanna said. "If Eldrack is using the same trick against all of them, we should know it so that we'll be ready."

"Exactly," Derek said. "Let's see what the book fairies can find for us."

Deanna went to the fairy librarian and asked

for books about the first four Mystical Guardians. The librarian called out to the book fairies who zipped from shelf to shelf and brought a stack of books to the twins' table.

The first book was old and tattered. When Deanna tapped the cover and said, "*Explanatum,*" it struggled to open its cover. "We would like to learn about the Mystical Guardians," she said. "We want to know about the level of their magical powers."

"Ah, yes," the book said in a raspy voice. "The Mystical Guardians are around here somewhere." The book's pages flipped back and forth. "Yes, here we go." The pages stopped fluttering, and the voice said,

*"The Mystical Guardians were selected by the great wizard Iszarre as agents of the Council of Dentrellius because the first Guardian demonstrated the greatest strength in all types of magic. The family was tested, and Iszarre confirmed that every generation would be very powerful.*

*The Mystical Guardians were given one assignment—defending Elestra against evil. Baladorn, the first Mystical Guardian did not have to wait long to battle against evil because Eldrack made his first appearance during*

*Baladorn's early years as a Guardian.*

*Baladorn led magical armies against Eldrack's forces thirteen times. His forces won ten battles. The other three times, both sides retreated from the battlefields. During the thirteenth battle, Baladorn's army nearly captured Eldrack, but the dark wizard escaped after he used a type of magical spell that had never been seen before."*

"I must rest now," the book said before slowly closing its cover.

"Thank you," Deanna said. "Please take it easy." She looked at Derek and said, "That book told us a lot, but we need to dig deeper."

"Yeah, I think that we should find out about the Council of Dentrellius," Derek said.

Deanna turned back to the books and said, "Can any of you tell us about the Council of Dentrellius?"

A small blue book hopped off of the stack and said, "I'm the book you need."

Deanna waved the wand and said, "Okay, we would like to know about the Council of Dentrellius and how it is connected to the Mystical Guardians."

The book sat silently on the table. Derek and

Deanna looked at each other. "What's going on?" Derek asked.

"*Explanatum,*" Deanna said. "Please tell us about the Council of Dentrellius."

The book remained quiet. Deanna tried to open the book and read the information herself. The book struggled to keep its cover closed. Derek tried to help her, but the book just got more wiggly.

The book escaped and tried to jump off of the table. Derek dove on top of it.

"Help, help," the book called out, hoping the librarian would come over and save it from the twins.

"You said that you had information about the Council of Dentrellius," Deanna said.

"I do," the book said while panting.

"Then tell us what you know," Deanna added.

"I can't do that," the book said. "The connection between the Mystical Guardians and the Council of Dentrellius is secret information. I cannot share this information with just anybody."

"Wait a minute," Derek said. "We are Mystical Guardians." The book made a sound like a snort that made him realize that the book didn't believe him. "That wand that Deanna is holding is the Wand of Ondarell. That's the wand of the

Mystical Guardians. It was given to us by Phillippe the Brave, our grandfather."

The book began mumbling very quietly to itself. "I see," it finally said. "Then I can give you this information, but only if you use the *Explanatum secretus* spell."

Deanna touched the book's cover and said, "*Explanatum secretus.*"

There was a large golden D on the cover which began to glow. A shimmering fountain of magical light shot up and created a curtain around the twins and the book.

The book opened to page 1 and a powerful voice said,

> "The Council of Dentrellius is a secret group of powerful wizards that was created after the little known attack on the Ruby Core that occurred in the years between the last king of Elestra and the reign of Barado. During this period, there was great confusion about who would rule the kingdom, and many wizards tried to take control.
>
> Iszarre saw that Elestra was in great danger and gathered the most powerful wizards in the realm to create a plan to fight against the rising tide of evil. Iszarre trusted the other

wizards on the Council, but he knew that they all had to protect their own people, so he sought out a family of wizards who would stand for all of Elestra.

Iszarre tested many wizards, and he finally chose one family that held great power. The wizards from this family became known as the Mystical Guardians. The first Mystical Guardian was Baladorn who did not have to wait long for a chance to fight against the evil that threatened Elestra.

Eldrack appeared days after King Barado's coronation and said that he challenged the new king's authority. Luckily, Iszarre was there and drove Eldrack away. Baladorn then led the forces of good against Eldrack for many years.

Baladorn was successful in keeping Eldrack on the run, and he nearly defeated Eldrack at the Battle of Pallendra.

Eldrack was able to escape after he used some sort of new magic that no one has ever been able to describe. Baladorn met with the Council and told them that he had no idea what Eldrack had done, and Iszarre was never able to figure out what happened.

After his close call at Pallendra, Eldrack changed his strategy. Instead of attacking Baladorn's armies, the dark wizard began *gathering followers and found powerful spells to put on places throughout Elestra. His spell of darkness over Amemnop was the most obvious example of this type of magical attack.*

*After Baladorn disappeared, the Mystical Guardians that followed him worked to stop Eldrack. Every one of the Guardians won many battles against Eldrack's armies, but it always seemed as if Eldrack studied their powers and finally found ways to capture each one."*

The book paused and then said, "That is all the information that I can give you here. Since you are Mystical Guardians, it may be best if I go with you. Call me when you need more information."

Before Derek or Deanna could ask anything else, the book burst into flames. A very thin column of fire shot up from the table and swirled around the twins. The ribbon of fire hit one of the moons on Derek's bracelet. The stone moon glowed for a few seconds, and then returned to normal. The fire was gone, and there was no evidence of the book on the table.

Derek looked down at his bracelet and said, "I guess you were right about bringing the bracelet, Deanna."

"Whoa," Deanna said. "I think we're going

to have to talk to Iszarre about the Council at some point. I want to know how many other wizards are working with him. If we have a lot of allies out there, it would be nice to know that."

"Why don't we go get some lunch and then come back and see if I can go down to the archive to meet with Gula Badu about that prophecy that Iszarre mentioned.

"Sounds good," Deanna said. They told the librarian that they were done with the books and walked out into the warmth of an Amemnop afternoon.

# Tarook

Lunch was disturbing. They had chosen a food cart that offered dishes from islands in the realm of Oceania. Deanna tried to eat a piece of fruit that swelled up like a balloon and exploded. Derek's sandwich bit him and then smeared mustard all over his face. They decided that they could wait to eat until they went back to the Grub Hut later.

Deanna was about to use a spell to clean the fruit's sticky juice off of them, but Derek said that he wanted to practice with the wand. Deanna told him the spell to use, and he pointed the wand at her.

"Wait a second," she yelled. "Before you use the spell on me, why don't you clean off that bush that has some of the fruit's goo on it."

Derek pointed the wand at the bush and said, "*Aquius!*" A shower of glittery dust blew against the bush. The sticky juice started to smoke, and the bush jumped out of the ground and ran around in circles on the street.

Derek put the wand back in Deanna's hand and said, "I think you better handle this."

She aimed the wand at the moving bush and said, "*Aquellius.*" A jet of water cleaned the bush off and cooled its burning leaves. It drooped over for a few seconds and then straightened up and returned to its place next to the sidewalk.

"You used a steam spell," Deanna said. "She waved the wand around and used the *Aquellius* spell again. Within seconds, all of the sticky juice was off of both of them. She used another spell to wash a warm wind over them to dry their clothes.

Once they were cleaned up, they headed back to the library. As they walked, Deanna said, "I don't get it, Derek. You seemed nervous trying the *Aquellius* spell, but you used a spell perfectly against Eldrack on Mt. Drasius."

"I've been reading about some spells early in the morning," Derek said. "That spell I used on Eldrack was actually a defensive spell. I don't know why, but I seem to be more interested in those."

"Well, whatever it was, it took care of Eldrack," Deanna said.

"Maybe he just didn't think I could do magic, so I caught him off guard," Derek replied.

"I think you need to give yourself more credit," Deanna added. "Maybe you're destined to be an expert in defensive spells."

"I guess so," Derek said. "I wouldn't be surprised if the Book of Spells could guide us to the spells we would do best."

Once they reached the library, Derek walked over to the librarian's desk and said, "I'd like to see Gula Badu, if possible."

"I'm sorry, young man," the librarian said. "Gula Badu is not in the Archive right now. She is meeting with the historians who make prophecies today. Perhaps she will be in tomorrow."

Deanna had come up behind Derek and heard what the librarian said. "That's too bad," she said. "Can we get books about Tarook, then?"

"Of course," the tiny librarian said. She called out to the book fairies who brought books about the snowhopper wizard to the same table that the twins had used earlier.

"I wanted to know a little more about Tarook," Deanna said. "If Eldrack captured him, he may have learned something about what Tarook had done with the moonstone. I want to know why Eldrack had the dragon capture him."

Deanna touched the first book and said, "*Explanatum.*" The book very carefully arranged itself so that it was exactly in the middle of the table. "Tell us about Tarook," Deanna said.

"Of course, Tarook, the wizard of the snowhoppers?" the book said.

"Yes, that Tarook," Derek said. "We want to know about him."

"About whom?" the book asked.

"Tarook," Deanna added.

"I'm sorry, who?" the book asked.

"Tarook, the snowhopper wizard," Deanna said.

"Never heard of him," the book said.

"But, you just said that you knew who he was," Derek said.

"Have we met?" the book asked.

Before Deanna or Derek could say anything else, the book on top of the pile jumped down and landed on the first book. The new book opened its cover and said, "You won't need the wand. I will be happy to give you the information you need. I'm afraid that this book under me is a little confused."

The other book was trying to say something, but it couldn't say anything with the new book sitting on it.

The new book said,

"Tarook was the greatest snowhopper wizard of the last five hundred years. He was known for his love of art and architecture. He built many structures that combined great art and magic. His Temple on Mt. Drasius was considered to be his greatest work. He also designed many other buildings throughout the lands of the snowhoppers and even some as far away as the Desert Realm.

There is much mystery surrounding many of Tarook's creations. For many years, no one has known the true purpose of his great Temple. Many of his other buildings seem to have secret areas and works of art that hide information that wizards may need to understand the types of magic that they must use in his buildings.

There are also lost structures that some people believe that Tarook built. A few of these have been found, but there is one that most people think is not real. There is a legend about a great underground palace built by Tarook. The legend says that the entrance to the palace is hidden and that it will be a place of great magic.

Some wizards believe that underground buildings could be very good places for magic because they could be closer to the Ruby Core, but others believe that underground structures would not be good because they would be blocked from the magical currents that float through the air in Elestra.

Many adventurers have searched throughout Elestra for this great lost Palace of Tarook, but none has ever found it.

The great wizard Iszarre was asked about the quest for the Palace of Tarook, and he said,

*"This story sounds ridiculous. A palace is something that a lot of people would go to. Someone would know where it is. Someone would have seen it being built. It's not like you can just find a huge underground area that can hold a palace."*

The book stopped reading from its own pages and said, "Does that help?"

"Yes, thank you," Deanna said. The book closed its cover, but continued to muffle the book below it.

"You know, Deanna, I'm pretty hungry," Derek said.

"Me too," Deanna replied. "Let's just head to Glabber's and get something to eat. We can talk about what we've learned here today."

They were curious to learn more about Tarook's other designs. It seemed like many people in Elestra thought that Tarook's work was important, especially the huge underground palace that seemed like a myth, even though many people spent years searching for it. They may have thought that the palace would hold a treasure that would make the one who found it rich.

After their experience at the food cart, they were hoping that Glabber had something recognizable cooking at the Grub Hut. As they walked along the boardwalk, they both felt like they had missed something important about Tarook and his lost palace in what the book had told them.

No matter how hard they thought, they couldn't figure it out. After all, like the book said, it wasn't like there was a huge underground area where Tarook could have built a palace. Or was there?

# Preview of Book 5

Derek and Deanna seek the fifth moonstone in *The Eye of the Red Dragon.*

The first chapter of the twins' fifth adventure in Elestra begins on the next page, and the story ends in the pages of *The Eye of the Red Dragon.*

# 1  Buzzy Little Baby

Derek and Deanna Hughes had trouble sleeping for the third straight night. After placing the fourth moonstone in the arch at the top of the Tower of the Moons three days earlier, they had awakened at the same time from separate dreams about their next adventure in Elestra with the words "The Eye of the Red Dragon" escaping their lips. They had become excited and nervous once they realized that they would come face to face with a real dragon. Again on this night, their dreams were filled with quick glimpses of dragons, volcanoes, and oddly enough, mushrooms.

The fifteen moons had all set, and the one Elestran sun was barely peeking above the horizon. Most of the residents of Amemnop were still warm in their beds. Derek pushed the huge window panels open to smell the fresh morning air. The sounds of the magical city caught his attention. He closed his eyes and tried to guess what he was hearing.

The first sound was a series of whooshes, with an occasional honking sound. "The giant geese from the goose-lot," Derek whispered to himself, thinking back on their ride on the huge birds. The next sound was a faint tinkling of running water, cutting through the light breeze. "The fountain," he smiled to himself.

The third sound he could make out was elusive. At first, he heard about ten clicks, then nothing. A few seconds later, twelve more clicks, then silence. Eight more clicks, but this time, a loud note from something that sounded like a kazoo. Derek opened his eyes and saw Deanna looking confused. "What was that?" she asked.

"I have no idea," Derek said. "I was trying to figure out the clicking sound. I think it's getting closer."

Derek was right—the next set of clicks was louder and deeper. He could not quite figure out what it was, but it reminded him of something. It was driving him crazy that he couldn't figure it out. The next clicks were even louder and sounded like something hitting wood.

"Tobungus!" Derek blurted out.

Derek and Deanna peered out the open window and finally found Tobungus, the mushroom man, walking along the wooden sidewalks in his cowboy boots. After a few steps, he stopped, looked down a narrow alley, and blew on a kazoo.

Derek did not want to yell out the window so early in the morning, so he rushed down the stairs, with Deanna right on his heels. She grabbed the Wand of Ondarell and her headband on the way out of the room.

A warm wind whipped their faces as they ran out of Glabber's Grub Hut. It was going to be a hot day in Amemnop.

They caught up with Tobungus, who did not seem to be in any sort of hurry on his strange rounds along the Amemnop store-fronts. "What are you doing?" Deanna asked.

"You wouldn't understand," Tobungus said quickly. He tried to push past the twins and continue his work.

"Try me," Deanna said, standing firm in front of him.

"Okay, okay," he said softly. "I need a new pair of shoes."

"What does that have to do with playing a kazoo?" Derek whispered, laughing under his breath. He should have known that this would have something to do with shoes. One of Tobungus' most treasured possessions was his shoe bag, which held dozens of pairs of shoes. Tobungus regularly changed his shoes in the middle of adventures to create the perfect outfit. Sometimes, it was a pair of cowboy boots, or running shoes, or even tap shoes.

"Just wait," Tobungus answered, looking around. "I suppose that you've never heard of kazoo honey." He saw their blank expressions. "No, I thought not. Well, purple chee-chee bees can't resist kazoo music. When they hear it, they bring their honey and deposit it on the kazoo. Anyway, this honey is more valuable than butter in Elestra. An ounce of purple chee-chee bee honey will fetch enough money for me to get a pair of cleats, with enough left over for a luxurious pair of slippers."

"Why are you looking for these bees here in town?" Deanna asked. "Wouldn't they be out in the country?"

"Well, they have been known to come into town, and I notice that the little girl over there was stung by one earlier," Tobungus said, pointing to his left.

Deanna looked around and saw no one. "Tobungus, what little girl?"

"See that blue mound over there," he answered, pointing to a five foot tall pile of bluish mud. "Chee-chee bee stings are not like most other bee stings. They cover the person who is stung with

a mound of, well, I guess you would call it goo."
He saw their worried expressions. "Don't worry, it
will wear off in a few hours."

"Tobungus," Deanna said worriedly, as a
loud buzzing started up after the latest kazoo blast.
Moments later, a four foot long bee floated out from
between the buildings to their right.

"Oh, look," Tobungus started, "it's a baby.
How cute."

"A baby?" Derek shouted.

Deanna grabbed her brother's hand and
pulled him down the street toward the blue mound.
"Let's get out of here," she yelled.

As they ran, Deanna whipped out the Wand
of Ondarell, muttered a few words and flicked it
toward the girl encased in chee-chee bee goo. A jet
of water hit the bluish mud and exposed a young
girl inside. Within seconds, the little girl was free,
running home to her parents.

Derek looked back and saw an adult bee,
about the size of a small house, gently depositing
several drops of honey on Tobungus' kazoo. He
stopped for a moment, looking at Tobungus and the
enormous bee in disbelief. Then, he turned and
kept running back to Glabber's without looking
back again.

Derek and Deanna found a table at the Grub

Hut and waited for breakfast, while keeping an eye out the window for the massive bees. After a while, the door burst open, and Tobungus walked in, with his short arms outstretched. "The shoe bag's about to get fatter," he exclaimed happily.

Glabber, the snake wizard and owner of the Grub Hut, slithered out to see what was going on. "Call me the Honey King," Tobungus roared. "I got a whole jug of purple chee-chee bee honey."

"My, my," Glabber hissed. "I'll pay the going rate for the whole supply." He slithered back into the kitchen and returned a few moments later with a black velvet bag which he dropped onto the counter.

Tobungus looked inside the bag, and then placed the jug of honey on the counter for Glabber to take. Glabber looked over to the twins, and hissed, "You two are in for a treat."

When their pancakes arrived, Glabber carefully placed one drop of the special honey on each plate.

"Wow," Derek said sarcastically, "Don't go overboard and give us too much or anything."

"You would not be prepared for more than one drop," Glabber said. "Chee-chee bee honey is almost like a magical elixir. You may know that normal honey is a good source of energy. Well, this is ten thousand times more powerful. It will give your bodies amazing power and energy."

Deanna dipped her fork in the honey drop and touched it to her tongue. Instantly, she felt a wave wash over her. Her body tingled. She seemed to hear and see better. Everything felt quicker.

"Now you see," Glabber hissed. "I will give each of you a small vial of the honey to take with you on your adventures, in case of emergencies." He slithered off after giving them their honey.

"When we get back from the picnic, I'm going to get my new shoes," Tobungus squealed.

"The picnic! It's today?" Deanna said excitedly, recalling that one of the King's messengers had appeared as a bird to invite them to a picnic in their honor. "I wonder when we'll have to leave to get to the King's picnic."

"Now should be fine," boomed a deep voice behind them. They turned to see Iszarre stowing his spatula wand in his belt.

"Will we be riding on one of the geese?" Deanna asked. She thought back to their goose ride to the Forest of Confusion on their way to finding the second moonstone in the Baroka Valley.

"No, we'll use magic," Iszarre answered.

"Are you trying to tell me that the geese that change from normal sized birds into giant flying transports are not magical?" Deanna asked.

"Oh, of course, you're right," Iszarre replied, "but we'll be using something new." He led them into the street.

"Something new?" Derek asked.

"Indeed," Iszarre said. "I've come up with my own method of travel that should prove interesting. Now, if that cat would just show up."

"Interesting? Wait! You've done this before, haven't you?" Derek asked.

Iszarre was searching up and down the street. "Iszarre," Derek said more loudly, "have you tried this new type of travel yet?"

"What," the wizard said absent-mindedly. "Oh, yes, I've already tried it, and it works perfectly." Just then, Zorell, the talking cat that traded insults with Tobungus constantly, ran up to the group.

"Will it just be you, or will the fleas be coming too?" Tobungus asked.

Pretending not to hear, Zorell said, "Is the King aware that we will be bringing mold spores with us."

"Can't this bickering wait until after lunch?" Deanna asked, with her hand resting on her wand. Tobungus and Zorell instantly became quiet.

Iszarre pulled out a thick rubber cord with a

ball at one end and something that looked like a cup at the other end. "Alright, the idea here is that this cup-like end will expand and act as a carriage. I'll throw the ball through a magical tunnel that I will open up, and the carriage will whip forward as the rubber snaps toward the ball. Easy! Nothing to it."

Iszarre pulled out his spatula and waved it at the air in front of him. A swirling patch of orange light grew larger and brighter, eventually opening into a tunnel that was so long that they couldn't see the other end. He touched the cup end of the rubber device, and it grew into a bowl at least five feet across. He threw the ball end through the tunnel, and jumped into bowl, with his spatula waving at the others. They all rose from the ground and landed with him in the bowl.

"You're sure you've done this before?" Derek asked, as the bowl began to move toward the tunnel.

"Yes," Iszarre answered. "Well, sort of. Actually, I haven't ridden in it. I used it to send a few bales of hay to a friend's donkey stables."

"Iszarre!" Derek yelled, as the bowl snapped suddenly into the tunnel. They were traveling faster than any of them could imagine. They could barely make out trees, rivers, and mountains passing under them. Then, everything was dark, as they flew across the space between Elestra and one of the moons.  Before they knew it, the light returned, and they were thrown out of the bowl, and into the upper branches of a huge tree.

"How do we get down?" Deanna groaned, looking at the ground, hundreds of feet below them. Before she could grab her wand and try some sort of levitation spell, several of the branches began to move.  The leafy arms grabbed the twins and their fellow travelers and carefully placed them on the ground.

Deanna's mouth was hanging open as she turned to say something to Iszarre.

"Thank you," the old wizard said, to the tree. "I'm starved.  Let's get to that picnic."

# Peekaboo Pepper Books

The line-up of Peekaboo Pepper Books is expanding quickly. We would like to take this opportunity to provide short previews of other upcoming titles in the *Guardians of Elestra* series.

*The Dark City: Guardians of Elestra #1*

Deanna and Derek follow their grandfather to Elestra where they learn that they are the last hope against a dark wizard in a race to collect the magical moonstones. They'll need all the help they can get from Tobungus, the tap-dancing mushroom man, Iszarre, the powerful wizard/fry cook, and Glabber, the snake wizard. Talking books, book fairies, flying coyote birdmen, devious hot peppers, and a short-tempered frog make their first adventure in Elestra one to remember.

*The Giants of the Baroka Valley: Guardians of Elestra #2*

Deanna and Derek set out on their second adventure in Elestra with Tobungus the mushroom man at their side. Along the way, they meet Zorell, a cat who has a hate/hate relationship with Tobungus, and ride a giant goose to the Baroka Valley. In the land where everything is huge, from the plants and animals to the grains of sand on a beach, they face off against Eldrack, fend off some sickening gong music, and sail down the River of the Dragon's Breath on an unusual boat. In the end, they are left with a new mystery and a plate of panpies (er, pancakes).

*The Desert of the Crescent Dunes: Guardians of Elestra #3*

Derek and Deanna venture outside of Magia for the first time. They find the Desert Realm to be hot and filled with Eldrack's minions. Their new friend Zorell joins them on the trip, much to Tobungus' dismay. It's a good thing he does, because his dancing proves to be a powerful weapon against Eldrack's army of tentacled sand beasts. Fortunately, the Desert Realm isn't without friends. They meet a resourceful girl named Dahlia who feeds them sugary lizard tails and reads prophecies woven in a hidden tapestry. After finding the entrance to a secret desert, they run into a mysterious statue who points out a solution to their problem. To escape from Eldrack's reach and return the moonstone to the arch, they must cross the Great Snort Pit in a boat scarred with bite marks that are frighteningly large.

*The Eye of the Red Dragon: Guardians of Elestra #5*

The twins and their friends accompany Iszarre to King Barado's castle for a picnic that ends with Iszarre arguing with a peach tree about giving him a second piece of fruit. Their search for the fifth moonstone starts with a trip to Tobungus' home, the Torallian Forest, so Zorell must meditate to find a happy place, and Tobungus needs to feed his shoes flipper juice to increase his dancing abilities. If Tobungus seems weird, his friend Rorrdoogo and the Mushroom wizard Bohootus are stranger yet. But, the real action takes place in the Dragon Realm where a young king finds his way, and his color, and an old dragon gets his mojo back. At the end of their adventure, as usual, Derek and Deanna are left with more questions than answers. Who was this friend who betrayed the older dragon, and where did all of the purple dragon wizards go?

*The Misty Peaks of Dentarus: Guardians of Elestra #6*

A trip to the mountains would be a nice way for Derek and Deanna to relax after their first five encounters with Eldrack. Unfortunately, these are the Antikrom Mountains where time occasionally goes in reverse, and where valleys are perfect places for an ambush by Eldrack's forces. The Iron Forest floats above the highest peaks, and the twins learn that sometimes the right jacket is all you need to fly. They meet their uncle, the yak farmer who insists that he must stay out of the family's battle against Eldrack. That's too bad because he could tip balance in their favor.

# Author Bio

Thom Jones is the author of the *Guardians of Elestra* series, as well as two forthcoming series, *Galactic Gourmets* (science fiction) and *The Adventures of Boron Jones* (superhero meets chemistry).

He has taught subjects including history, atmospheric science, and criminology at various colleges. What he loves to do most, though, is work with kids, which he does at the crime scene camps he runs. He began writing the *Guardians of Elestra* stories in 2004 for his two sons. The stories evolved, and Tobungus got stranger over the years. He finally decided to start Peekaboo Pepper Books and publish the stories with the view that kids are smart and funny, and that they are more engaged by somewhat challenging vocabulary and mysteries woven throughout the stories they read.

He lives in the Adirondacks with his wife Linda and their three children, Galen, Aidan, and Dinara. He is extremely lucky to have such wonderful editors in Linda, Galen, and Aidan, who have found too many errors to count and have come up with fantastic ideas, even when they don't know it.

51690479R00084

Made in the USA
San Bernardino, CA
29 July 2017